The Cupid Crisis

LISA BUSCEMI REISS

Literary Crush Publishing

Sweet Romance. Forever Love.

Literary Crush Publishing
75 E Center St
PO Box 451
Springville, UT 84663

The Cupid Crisis

For information about special discounts for bulk purchases, please contact Literary Crush Publishing: Contact@literarycrushpublishing.com

Literary Crush Publishing can bring authors to your live event. For more information or to book an event, contact us at: contact@literarycrushpublishing.com

Typesetting: Brookie Cowles

Cover Design: Blue Water Books

A CIP record for this book is available from the Library of Congress Cataloging-in-Publication Data

ISBN: 978-0-9984484-5-9

ISBN: 978-0-9984484-6-6 (eBook)

For Mike, Steven, and Julianna. My World.

CHAPTER ONE

CUPID'S STALKING ME. I can feel it. He's itching to make a love match, and there's a big, round target on my butt. He's already shot a few of my friends. You should see them. They walk around all lovey-dovey-eyed like lovesick puppies.

But I'm too clever for him, even when I feel him above me, pointing that stupid arrow of his.

I might feel differently if love didn't stink, but it does. I know that firsthand. Now, I don't trust *any* guy, let alone Cupid—an ancient cherub who doesn't even wear pants.

Lately, it's been hard to avoid Cupid. He's plastered all over the walls of my school, thanks to The Cupid Connection—our school's Valentine's dance. His beady eyes follow me as I walk to algebra, or when I'm standing in line at the cafeteria waiting for a slice of pizza.

Did I mention it's only January? There's still three more weeks until Valentine's Day!

The dance committee even came up with Cupid-grams as a fundraiser. A male student, dressed as Cupid (in a toga!), delivers prepaid, love-dripped messages to students in class. Gag. Receiving a Cupid-gram in the middle of class and having a Nerf dart flung at me with a sappy message? That would kill me even more than what happened during Christmas break.

Which was also Cupid's fault, by the way.

So, despite whatever messages he puts out there about love being so great and special, I know the truth. Love only brings heartache.

I'm onto the chubby god of love.

Right now, he's working through my best friend, Olivia. We're in my room, sitting on my bed.

"*Pleeease?*" Liv says now, with more pep in her voice than usual. "Let me introduce you to one of my friends from science lab. Then you can go to the dance. It'll be so good for you to get out there again and…" she winces, "date."

I shake my head, holding firm. I see right through her. I know Cupid's using her to work his magic.

"Claire," she says softly. "It's been nearly a month since the breakup."

"I told you," I said. "No guys. No dating. I don't even want to go."

"But you said—"

"I changed my mind." I wish I had never told Liv I'd go. It was post-breakup after all, so I was out of my mind. At the time, I thought it might be a good idea to go because I'd show Josh I was moving on. Also, I'd show Briana that I didn't care that she broke the Girl Code—at Christmastime no less, not to mention wrecking the lifelong friendship she, Liv, and I shared—and stole him from me.

Stole. Him. From. Me.

"Besides," I add. "Didn't I go through enough at the last party I attended? Don't you feel sorry for me, even this much?" I hold up two fingers, showing her about half an inch.

My heart hurts just thinking about December 27th. That was the day I lost my boyfriend, my best friend, and my lunch all at the same time.

Liv leans in, about a millimeter from my face. "But this is different, Claire. This isn't a party at Briana's house or a sophomore dance. This is a whole school party. She probably won't even be there. She hates school things. So does—"

I hold up a hand. "Don't even say his name." Every letter of it stabs me in the heart like one of Cupid's dumb arrows.

"I just think it'll be great. Because if *he* does go, it will totally show him that you're over him."

She's got a point. And that was my original intention. But do I really need to see him if he's there with her? It's bad enough that I see them in the hallways at school. Each time I do, memories of that night flood my mind.

Briana's parents were in Barbados for a few days, and Briana told her parents she would stay at my house, which she did, except for this one night. Her house was jam-packed with people from school because our get-together began with a few friends and social media helped turn it into Party Central. I knew that Liv and I would have to return the next day to help clean up and wipe away any and all evidence of the party.

I had to get home or I'd miss my ten o'clock curfew, so Liv and I went in search of Josh and Briana. We scanned the rooms one by one until we came to the upstairs bathroom. I was the one who opened the slightly ajar door. Liv gasped beside me. In front of me were Josh and Briana, leaning on the sink. His arms were wrapped around her waist, and her arms were wrapped around his neck. They were making out. Making out! My boyfriend! And my best friend!

After my feet finally listened to my brain, I threw the promise ring Josh gave me at them, and then I ran out of the house. Liv followed. I can't remember much after that except that I tossed my cookies into a bush.

I shake off the memory. How could I have been so stupid?

How had I not seen that coming?

So the chances of me going to this stupid Cupid Connection

dance, especially with someone new? Um, yeah, that'd be a big fat *zero*. And falling in love again? I'm avoiding *that* like my grandma's liver and onions.

Liv's still talking about the dance. She's got a running list of pros, and she's firing them off to me one by one, counting on her fingers. "One," she says. "It's going to prove to them both that you're so over them. Two, it gets you out, meeting other people. Three, it'll be fun. There'll be punch! Music! Dancing! Those are bullets A, B, and C," she adds.

I rub the bridge of my nose. Just discussing this is giving me a dull headache.

"You'll show up late and looking *hot*," she adds. "Like what Alyssa did on that episode of The Bachelor where she wanted to make Franco jealous."

Josh and I used to watch that show together. I take a deep breath and let it out slowly as Liv goes on to her bonus point 3-A, which is that she will be there.

"Look, Liv," I say. "You know I love you. I do. And I know you want me to go, but how can I? How can I watch them dance and make out and be a happy couple when I'm standing there holding up the wall?"

"That's just it. You'd have a date."

"A fake date."

"Josh won't know that."

I'm still so sad over the whole thing I don't even care that she just said his name again.

"I know you were hurt," Liv adds. "But it's old news now, Claire."

I straighten my shoulders. "Not to me it isn't. And if it happened to you, you'd feel the same way." I know this isn't exactly true. The closest she's ever been to being this hurt was when she found out Jason didn't like her back. But then, five minutes later, Dillon asked her out. The list of guys who like her is long. She can take her pick of any one of them if she wants.

"I'm sorry," Liv says. "I know how hurt you are. But we've still got three weeks before the dance, and I don't know, maybe you'll feel better by then. Things can change."

Dance, dance, dance. It's all she talks about these days.

"I'm not dating anyone. Read my lips. Not. Dating. Any. One."

Liv smirks and I get a chill that goes from my scalp to my pedicure-needing toes. "Why are you looking at me that way? Cut it out."

Her smile widens. "Make a wish."

"Why?"

"Can't you feel it? There's magic in the air. I think Cupid's watching over us right now."

"Ugh, you feel that, too?" I glance around the room as if I'll see him hovering above us or something.

"Yes! He wants to make sure we have dates to the dance. It's in his honor, after all."

I look at Liv again. "Stop that. I was kidding. There's no magic. Cupid's not even real. Besides, you don't even have a date, so...."

"Yet." She smiles wider, wagging her eyebrows. Sure, Liv can go with any guy. They line up for her. "And you blame Cupid for everything, so why can't I? Just humor me, will ya? It can't hurt."

"Oh my gosh, Liv. Really?"

"Yes. Wish for a new, awesome boyfriend, one who will treat you like a princess. No, like a queen. Not like you-know-who. It's time for a good change."

"Can't I wish for, like, a million dollars? Or a new wardrobe? Or...."

"No. Shush." Liv thinks a moment, and then her face lights up. "Ooh! There's this guy in my tech class. He can help make Josh—I mean *him*—jealous. He's so cute, and I think he's single. It'll drive you-know-who crazy. His name's Edwin. Or is it Gary? No, wait. Jordon."

I take a deep breath and hold it before letting it out. "Liv," I say. "Why aren't you getting it?"

"Because I love you." She grins, toothy and wide. I know she's trying to wear me down but I hold fast to my frown.

"Have you forgotten the last time you tried to set me up?" I finally say.

Liv giggles. "*Not* funny," I tell her as my face gets hot. "So, yeah, no." After a pause I feel bad. I don't want her to be upset. "Look," I add. "Maybe I'll help you and the committee set up, make flyers, whatever. I might even help make cutesy chocolate heart lollipop favors, but no dates."

She perks back up. "Okay! But make the wish. Maybe it'll give you good mojo or something."

"Mojo?" I shake my head. "You and your superstitions."

"It's good energy. Karma and all that. And I only say these things because I want someone to treat you like a goddess. Unlike someone who never even gave you flowers, or who gave you a crummy card for Valentine's Day last year and not even one piece of candy."

I know exactly what she's referencing. The card I've kept from Josh. The only card he's ever given me. It has a silhouette of Cupid on the front. He's about to fire his bow, and inside, in bold print, it says, '*I'm aiming straight for your heart. Happy Valentine's Day.*' All Josh wrote was his name at the very bottom. He didn't even write, 'Love'.

Liv has a point. Making Josh jealous won't change things, but it'll make me feel a little better, that's for sure.

She reaches for my hand now. "Seriously, Claire," she insists, "you're such a good person. You deserve all the best things in life. Especially love and happiness. I mean it."

I tear up and swallow the lump in my throat.

"Now close your eyes. Think hard of one thing you truly want. But don't wish to obliterate you-know-who. That's not good karma."

"That's going to be hard then," I say, laughing, but against my better judgement, I make a wish. From deep, deep down, I dig it up. Like Liv said, wishing for revenge isn't good karma so that's out. And wishing for a new boyfriend is not what I want. So I do make the obvious choice and wish for Josh back, for things to be the way they were before he hooked up with Briana.

After a few moments, I open my eyes. I don't know what I was expecting, but everything's the same. Except Liv's grinning like a deranged clown. "See?" she says. "Painless."

"I didn't wish for anything spectacular," I start to say, and suddenly, I feel guilty. She'd be disappointed if she knew my wish.

Beaming in approval, she holds up one hand. "Don't tell me, or it won't come true." Then she gets up and pulls her coat on. "I'll talk to you tomorrow. Let the mojo begin!"

CHAPTER TWO

AFTER LIV LEAVES, I try to focus on my homework. But with all the talk of wishing and mojos and love, I can't concentrate.

It keeps reminding me of Josh, and the sadness weighs me down. His face keeps popping onto the pages in my history book. His image dances above the words describing nineteenth-century European government. At first, he's as cute as the day I met him a year ago, but then I see Briana's face on the opposite page. I imagine Cupid now, the one from Josh's card, shooting his arrow straight into Josh's butt. Then he flings one into Briana's, and they look at each other, run together with arms outstretched, and start to make out right between the French Revolution and the execution of Louis XVI.

I slam the book shut. "Go love yourself, Cupid." I hope I squashed all three of them like bugs. *What a waste of a wish. How could I want Josh back? If that happened, all he'd do is hurt me again.*

I grab my phone, pop in my ear buds, and hit *play* on what I've dubbed my personal anti-love anthem. This song's really old, from the 80s, but when I recently discovered it on YouTube, I knew it fit me. If I could have a personal life theme song, it'd be this one. I turn up the volume and begin to sing along, especially when the chorus comes on: *"Love stinks! Yeah, yeah! Love stinks!"*

But even that doesn't make me feel any better. So I watch TV, clicking through endless channels. There are some days when, even though it's been weeks since our breakup, every guy makes me think of Josh, even the news anchor who's a hundred and twenty with fake teeth.

Today's one of those days.

I'm about to go downstairs to see if dinner is ready, even though I'm not hungry, when my cell phone rings. It's probably Liv.

Except it isn't. The caller ID says it's a number I don't recognize.

I let it go to voicemail. Liv probably already has Edwin/Gary/Jordon calling me. This annoys me all over again, and I think it's time to seriously consider relocating to the South Pole. Or at least Ohio.

Once the message is recorded, the alert icon pops up. I'm curious. It won't hurt to hear the pathetic set-up attempt by one Ms. Olivia Cruz, so I press *play* and prepare to be amused.

"Oh, hey," says the caller. It's a guy, and his voice is soft, like he's cool but not trying too hard.

"Uh, it was really great to meet you," he continues.

Meet me? Okay, good one, Liv.

"…and I'm just, you know, calling to see if you want to hang out. I don't know, maybe we could meet up at the mall and decide from there? Or we can meet someplace else if that's too lame…. Sorry, I've never called anyone I just met before. So, uh, anyway, I'll be at the mall Tuesday at four. If you want. Because that's one of my days off from work. Anyway, I'll be at the food court. Maybe I'll see you there? Four o'clock? If not, another time's good, too. Ugh, I hate leaving messages. Okay. Bye."

Lame. Wait until I talk to Liv. This has her written all over it. I replay the message so I can maybe figure out who this guy is and be a step ahead of her. But after listening three times, I don't recognize his voice.

Whatever. I save the message and call her.

"Hello?"

"Nice try, Liv."

"Huh?"

"The phone call."

"What phone call?"

"The one I just got on my cell. From the guy."

"What guy?"

I give her a moment. She'll give in if I wait long enough. And I can wait all night.

"Ooh!" she says making me jump. "Maybe that was a result of your wish! Did you wish for a guy to call you? Oh my gosh, Claire!"

"No! Calm down, Liv," I say. "So, that wasn't Edwin/Gary/Jordon?"

"I don't work that fast." She laughs. "What did he say?"

Okay, this is weird because she sounds like she's being truthful. Normally, Liv can't tell a lie very well. She gets all red in the face and giggles. I can't see her, of course, but right now, there's not even a snicker on her end.

"Maybe it was a wrong number," I say. I guess it's possible. A huge coincidence, but possible. I don't leave my name on my outgoing voicemail message or use my own voice. It's the default recording that my phone came with. My mind races back to all the things the caller said: *just met...doesn't normally do this...meet up at the mall....*

"Never mind," I say. "Forget it. But that was weird."

"It was. Okay, well, I've got to get back to my homework. I'll see you tomorrow?"

"Yeah. See you."

"Keep me posted if he calls back! Oh, and don't forget we have a dance committee meeting on Monday after school."

"Yeah, yeah, I'll be there." Why did I volunteer for that?

We hang up. I stare at the phone. Is she really telling me the truth about the phone call? Or did she just put one over me?

I can picture her right now, laughing into her hand. I picture Cupid with her holding his bow. *"We got her good!"* they'd both be saying while high-fiving each other. *"Yes! She'll meet this guy at the mall,"* Liv would say. *"He'll ask her out and—bonus!—she'll go to the dance and go back to being the Claire we all know and love!"*

Yeah, and this guy's probably a moth-eating troll.

"I'm onto you, Cupid!" I yell toward my ceiling. "Did you hear me?" I know. It seems strange to talk to an imaginary Cupid. But I'm superstitious, too, and like I said, I know he's stalking me.

I plop onto my bed, face first. Now I'm angry all over again, wondering to what lengths Liv will go to see me date someone new.

I don't want a new boyfriend. I want Josh. And I can't even tell my best friend about the wish I made. She'd be all: *"Oh-em-gee, Claire, you need to get over him. It's time to move on, blah, blah, blah."*

Maybe she is right that it's old news. It has been weeks since Christmas break. Everyone seems to be moving on but me. And maybe things weren't always perfect with Josh, but that doesn't mean I want to meet someone else. I'm not going to the mall. I'm not falling for Liv's evil plan.

I'm. Not. Going.

I'll take the 3:35 bus to the mall on Tuesday.

CHAPTER THREE

IT'S FINALLY TUESDAY. For the past three days, all I've been able to think about is this caller guy. If it wasn't Liv trying to set me up, if it's totally legit, what could his story be?

During Biology I come up with a possible scenario in my head: he's tall and cute and has dark, wavy hair and long eyelashes. Bulging muscles in his upper arms, the kind that you can see through a t-shirt. He meets the girl he was calling at a friend's house. It's not a party-party, maybe it's a football game get-together, and his friend introduces him to her. She's kind of plain. And she has buck teeth and a hairy wart on her nose. Okay, maybe not, but she's way more plain than I am.

Anyway, he tries to strike up a conversation with her, first about the football game and then about school, and she soon seems bored. Between taking bites of pretzel squares and Cheez-Its, he awkwardly (but sweetly) asks her out. That's when things take a weird turn for the worse because she's trying to catch the eye of her friend across the room. So, in order to get him to leave her alone, she scribbles a random phone number (which happens to be mine) on a napkin. "Sure, call me," she says quickly and leaves him standing there with a handful of Cheez-Its and a crumbled-up and now orange-speckled napkin in his sweaty hand.

That would be so mean, so I hope that's *not* what happened. But thinking this way helps me to feel like it'd be okay to check out this guy at the mall later today. Like, maybe he needs a break. Poor guy.

The bell rings, and I collect my books. Liv meets me at the doorway, and we walk down the hall together. We dodge students as if we're in a living video game.

"I wish you'd sit with us during lunch," Liv says. She's been asking almost every day since the breakup. So far, I've managed to avoid Josh and Briana for the most part. I mean, I can't avoid them altogether, but whenever I see them, I make a sharp turn in the opposite direction, or look down at the floor as I walk, or pretend to talk to Liv. I also usually eat in the girls' room in the art wing because that one's usually empty. Gross, I know, but it beats watching them make out over yesterday's meatloaf. And since they're both in our lunch class, well, it's easier to avoid them than to confront the issue.

"Maybe soon," I say. Liv looks sad. She's got other friends to sit with, so I'm flattered she misses me and wants me there. "I need more time."

We part ways. Liv goes to math, I've got study hall. On the way toward my classroom, I stop to get a bottle of water at the vending machine outside the cafeteria.

There's a line, so I wait. That's when I see him. Josh is three people ahead of me. My eyes follow his hairline down the curve of his muscular neck. He's wearing a gold chain, one I've never seen before. I bet he got it for his birthday. Probably from Briana.

The line moves, but I don't, so the kid behind me gives me a nudge and says, "Hey, move already." At that, Josh turns and we lock eyes.

He nods to me. At first, I'm frozen, and then I manage to

swallow hard. Josh looks away and the spell is broken. The kid pokes me in the arm.

"I'm going!" I say probably a bit too loudly. But I wait for Josh to be gone before I move again.

This is how it is and who I am now. Rattled by every sight of him. Pushed to remember happy times, even as the end stings.

I spend all of study hall thinking of his face. His hair. How it used to be having a boyfriend. How I always had him to talk to.

After our last class, I'm headed toward my locker, while trying to ignore Jimmy Muller and Brandon Woods, who are behind me cat-calling at all the girls, including me. I turn and give them the stink-eye over my shoulder. All guys are dogs. No, wait. Scratch that. Dogs are warm, loyal and sweet. Guys are stomach viruses.

I meet up with Liv at her locker.

"Hey," she says.

"Hey."

This is the umpteenth time today that I've seen her, and for the umpteenth time she's straight-faced and showing not one sign of having hatched a plan. By now, I'm totally confused and worn out anyway.

"I saw him today. We were, like, three feet apart. He said hey. Sort of. It was just…hard."

She frowns and gives me a one-armed hug. "I'm sorry," she says into my hair. When she pulls back, she digs around in her purse. "Here." She pulls out a Hershey bar, my favorite.

"Thanks."

I open the candy bar, take a bite, and then hold it out, offering her some. She opens her mouth, and I pop a piece in while she's exchanging books from her locker.

I'm glad she's my friend. She's always been there for me. She always listened to me whenever I spoke about Josh and even when I complained about him. Briana was there for me then, too, but not like Liv. Now I know why.

"It'll get easier, I promise," Liv says, breaking into my

thoughts. She closes the locker door and faces me. "Especially when you meet someone new, even though you don't want to hear that."

My thoughts travel to the guy who left me the accidental message the other night. Could he be a "someone new"? I decide to test her again.

"Hey, what are you doing after school today?" I ask.

Liv shrugs. "I don't know, probably just homework. Why?"

"No reason. I thought I'd ask if you wanted to go somewhere. Anywhere. Being it's Tuesday and all." I look at the candy bar. Rip the wrapper a little more and stall a moment. "How about the mall?"

"What does Tuesday have to do with anything?" she says. "And I don't have any money. I'll have babysitting money after the weekend if you want to wait."

Huh. She doesn't seem even half a percent guilty of any type of masterminding. I'm totally stumped. "Okay," I say. "Maybe I'll call you later? After homework?"

"Okay," she says, and we part ways to find our buses out front.

All the way home, I stare out the bus window, finishing my chocolate bar one square at a time and thinking about going to the mall today if only to keep my mind off of Josh and the constant hurt I feel deep down in my belly. I tell myself that I don't have to talk to this phone-call guy if I don't want to. He doesn't know me or that I'm coming, especially if it was a mistake on his part. And I'm just going to look for a guy waiting alone who seems like he's waiting for someone. Just to see if the call was authentic.

But then what?

I consider the list of pros and cons I wrote in my notebook while in math class:

Pro: Maybe he's really cute and super sweet.

Con: Liv set this up and will never let me live it down, especially if it works out.

Pro: I don't think she did.

Con: He called someone else.

Pro: If we meet, he might like me.

Con: He might like me. I don't want a new boyfriend.

Pro: It might be love at first sight

Con: Love is blind. And sometimes it's dumb.

Pro: Today's the 27th, one month to the day that Josh and I broke up. Maybe something new and happy can happen to replace the bad.

Con: It's the anniversary of our breakup. :(

Pro: Maybe he's cute.

Con: He's a guy. He'll eventually cheat on me.

Pro: He's not *him*.

Con: He's not *him*.

Sigh.

CHAPTER FOUR

BY THE TIME I get home from school on Tuesday, my thoughts are a tangled, jumbled mess. I know I should get over Josh. And I know I should forget the caller guy. But I can't seem to do either.

I'm so deep in thought I don't even realize my brother Evan is saying something to me until he huffs.

"What?" I ask, after I send a quick text to Mom, who's still at work at the hair salon, to tell her I'm going to the mall to look for a new pair of boots since my suede ones got ruined by the snow last winter. It's not a total lie. I really need new boots, and I just got a few gift cards for Christmas.

"Did you even hear me?" Evan says as he reaches for the milk carton from the fridge for his typical after-school snack of Oreos and ice-cold milk.

"No. Sorry."

He makes a clucking sound with his tongue. "I asked you about…" he lowers his voice, *"Leah."*

"Why are you whispering?" I ask. "No one's here, you dork."

His face blotches up, and he shuffles from foot to foot. "I don't know." For a younger brother, he's usually super annoying, but right now I think he's being super adorable. Especially since he just turned thirteen and he's really awkward around any female he encounters.

"Wow," I tease. "You're in *love*, aren't you?" He puts the milk back and grabs his cookies and the mug, and I imagine Cupid again, this time aiming an arrow at Evan's chest. I see it vividly in my mind. He pulls back the arrow. Aims. Closes one eye; he's about to let it sail. I want to push my little brother out of the line of fire and scream, "Look out!" but I manage to refrain.

Besides, Evan looks pissed at me now, so if I did that, he'd probably punch me.

"Shut up. I am not." He turns to leave, but I grab his arm. A little milk spills on the tiled floor.

"Sorry," I say. "I didn't mean to embarrass you. What did you want to know?" I wait, and then I add, "I'm being serious, I promise."

He lowers his voice again. "How do I ask her out?"

Dating and relationships are the last things I want to talk about right now. But for Evan, and only for a moment or two, I let the wall down.

I look back at Evan. "Just ask her out."

"But what do I *say*?"

"I don't know. Just be yourself." This was always the advice given to me from both my mom and my dad, who incidentally have been together and completely in love for twenty years now. It's something I used to aspire to. Now, I doubt it's possible for me. Maybe they have some secret magic I don't know about.

"That's the problem," he says. "Last time I tried to talk to her, I went to her lunch table and tapped her shoulder. It took all day for me to get up the courage to do that. When she turned around, I just stood there with my jaw hanging open like a puppet. Then I sort of squeaked half a word out. Everyone laughed. It was humiliating."

I fight the urge to smile by biting my lip. I'm not even being mean about it. I know how sweet this must've seemed to her, but I also know how embarrassed he must've felt.

"I bet she thought you were cute."

"I don't want to be cute," he says. "I want her to think I'm hot."

Now I do laugh.

"Forget it!" he says and leaves me standing there.

"Evan, wait," I say, rushing after him.

He stops, and so do I, but he doesn't turn around to face me. "What?"

"Just try talking to her again. Say, 'Hey,' and she'll say, 'Hey' back, and then you say, 'I'm Evan,' and she'll say she's Leah, and then you say something else—anything—like, 'What did you think of Mr. Sander's assembly speech last week?' Just make simple conversation." I place my hand on his shoulder to show him I mean it. "It'll be okay, Evan, I know it. And I didn't mean to laugh just now. I think you're sweet, and I'm willing to bet she will, too. You're an awesome guy, and if she likes you back, she'll show it right away. Just be you. Okay?"

"Yeah. Thanks," he says, still not turning around. "I'll try, but it's not that easy, like how it is for you."

He goes off to his bedroom. He has no idea how completely untrue that is for me now or what happened last month. He only knows what everyone else does: that Josh and I broke up, and that I've been sad for weeks, and how I never wanted to talk about it, not even to Mom or Dad.

He also has no idea I'm about to see a guy in person who called my cell phone by mistake and that I'm probably about to set myself up for another let-down. And speaking of that, it's almost 3:00, so if I want to be there by 4:00, I'll have to change my outfit and fix my hair now.

In my room, I pick out a pair of jeans and a sweater. Nothing too fancy. Definitely mall-worthy, but also slightly more. As I dress, I go over everything in my head again: I'm just going to see if he shows up, that's all. Then I'll take it from there. Feel the situation out. No promises, no worries.

Then I pause for a moment. Wait. How will I know who he is? I'll have to search for someone sitting alone by the food court. If he's not there, it'll be a huge possibility Liv *was* behind it and she will have called it off because I seemed too suspicious today at school.

I'll be on the lookout for her, too. And for a good deal on boots.

Because that's all I'm really going for.

CHAPTER FIVE

A FEW MINUTES LATER, I call out to Evan, "I'm going to the mall! Be home soon!" He mumbles something that sounds like acknowledgement above the sounds of the video game he's playing on his X-Box. I leave a quick note for Mom, grab my jacket and purse, and go.

I'm so nervous. I take my bike to the bus stop on Main and lock it into the rack. The Number 11 bus goes to and from the mall once per hour, and I've taken it a bazillion times, so I've already worked it out that, if this guy isn't there, or is super creepy or ninety-seven years old, or if Liv's standing on the side-lines snickering into her hand, I'll have to kill time for about 45 minutes till the next outgoing bus home. Not too bad.

I climb into the bus, sweaty palms and all, and by the time we pull into the mall parking lot twenty minutes later, my belly's filled with butterflies. *Stop it,* I tell myself as I step off the bottom step. *You're just looking around. Checking things out.*

When I pull out my phone to keep busy, I notice today's date again. January 27th. I open an app and scroll funny memes to keep my mind off of Josh, and off the one-month anniversary of our break-up. But no matter how funny the pictures of chubby cats and pop- culture icons are, images of him kissing Briana at that party keep popping into my brain.

A few moments later, the bus stops and I step out into the brisk air. I head inside the mall through the double glass doors, and when I do, Cupids attack me. Well, not literally, but it looks like Valentine's Day threw up everywhere. I shrug off my jacket and fling it over my arm. I take my time walking past the stores, every one of them decorated wall-to-wall with dangling hearts, Cupids, and flowers.

I stop at Walker's, the shoe store, and see a few cute pairs of boots and force myself to listen to the sales girl drone on and on about leather this, and sturdy that, but I'm busy thinking about the caller. I check the time on my cell. It's 3:55. I thank the sales-girl, who may still be talking, step out of the store, and head toward the food court.

I look into every face I pass. Looking for Liv. Looking for a guy who seems to be waiting for a date. I see moms with daughters. Couples, young and old. A guy walking past, talking on his cell phone. Even a security guard.

As I walk toward the food court, I pass Starbucks and get a whiff of rich, roasted coffee beans. I should just treat myself to a mocha latte and go home. But as I get closer to the food court, I smell a combo of Italian, Chinese, and American buffet, and the tables are about half-filled with diners. Now I'm too curious to leave, coffee luring me or not.

I gaze about the area, pretending to not be looking at anything specific. I chew the inside of my lip, attempting to keep a blank face. Look around again. Check my phone. Put it back in my pocket. Take it out again. Read menus. Pretend to look for a place to sit because, yes, I eat alone at the mall all the time.

I see families. Friends. Another security guard. But no one is sitting alone.

I sigh. This was dumb. And totally abnormal. I decide to leave. But first I'll get myself that mocha latte so it won't be a total waste of time. Yeah, that's what I'll do. And purchase a new pair of boots. Because why not.

I'm about to turn and go back when I notice a young guy, about my age, sitting alone in the food court near Nick's Pizza, and looking down at his phone.

And he's cute.

I slip into Victoria's Secret and pretend to look at the bras, spread out on a table display, but really, I'm trying to see what this guy's doing and waiting to see if someone joins him. But for, like, *ever*, he sits there by himself. He's not eating, not drinking, and nobody joins him. I'm not sure what to do. Go out there? Say something? What did I really think would happen anyway? This *was* crazy.

I take out my cell again. I need to call Liv. I'll confess why I'm here, see how she reacts. But then I get an idea. I'll dial the mysterious caller's number and see if this guy picks up. I search his number and dial but I press *67 first so my number doesn't show up.

It rings once on my end. The guy looks down at his phone, touches the screen, and then puts the phone to his ear. "Hello?" he says.

I panic and hang up. He pulls his phone from his ear and stares at it. Then he shrugs and touches the screen again.

It *is* him!

Just then, I get a tap on my shoulder. I gasp, and swing around. My phone, along with some of the bras, goes flying.

The salesgirl yelps and puts a hand on her chest. "Are you okay?" she asks. "You scared me!"

I pick up my phone and reattach the battery. Then I pick up a couple of bras and place them back on the table. "I'm so sorry," I say, my face warm. "You scared me, too."

She picks up another bra and says, "Sorry. Did you need help with something? I noticed you were looking a while."

"Oh, no thanks. I've got tons of bras."

Ugh. Did I just say that? I scurry out before I'm arrested on suspicion of shoplifting B-cups. As I cross the threshold, I bump into a woman leaving at the same time as me. "Oh, sorry," we both say over the sound of the store alarm going off. The salesgirl approaches the woman and begins asking her questions. I wonder if she shoplifted. *Wow, I'd never do that,* I think as I make a sharp right and head to the food court.

When I get there, I see that the guy's still sitting by the Italian booth, looking at his phone. Now that I think about it, I feel awful. Obviously, it's not Liv's doing. And it's bad enough the girl he thought he'd meet didn't show up, but now I just prank-called him. What was I thinking by coming here? I don't know what to do.

Coffee. That's it, just get coffee and go home. Call it a loss.

Maybe later I'll text him and tell him what happened. No harm done because, really, he took a chance to meet her here. And she never answered.

But *I* could have answered. I could have told him about his mistake, his wrong number, and then he wouldn't be sitting here alone, probably feeling like a loser because she never showed up.

But it's not my fault she gave him a bum number, and it's not my fault he came without knowing if she would show up, right?

I could do this to myself forever. I head to Starbucks, and on the way, my cell rings, making me jump. For a split second, I hold my breath, thinking it might be him, but it's not. It's Liv.

"Where are you?" she says after I pick up.

"At the mall. Remember?"

"I thought you'd wait for me to…oh…are you getting a dress for the party? Was that why you wanted to go to the mall? Check out Abercrombie. Or Bloomindales. I love Bloomies! And they always have great sales. What color do you think you'd wear? Are you considering going now? I hope so! Oh, I need a dress, too. Are you still there?"

"Yeah." I take a breath. "Listen, there's something I have to tell you, and no, it's not about the dance." I step into the coffee shop and stand in line.

"What's up?" she asks, and I can hear her crunching something. Probably Cool Ranch Doritos.

"I'll tell you when I see you. I'm about to order a coffee. You'll be home? Maybe I'll just stop by."

"Okay."

Huh. So maybe this whole thing wasn't Liv's idea and it really was a wrong number. Now I feel stupid. Stupid and mean. We hang up, and as I inch my way up in line, I tell myself I was wrong to come here. Seriously. What was I going to do, ask the guy out? I gave up dating, so why did I let my curiosity get to me that way? This is Cupid's fault. Or maybe it's his idea of a joke, since I wished for Josh back.

And I didn't even get boots.

I decide that, when I get home, I'll text the guy and tell him he had the wrong number. Case closed. Move on.

Just then, a scent fills my nose. It's a guy's cologne, and it's the same one Josh wears. My shoulders deflate, and all the air escapes from my lungs like a punctured tire. I reconsider my coffee, and I'm about to leave when someone taps my arm. "Um, excuse me?"

I turn around.

It's him.

The cute guy from the phone call.

My mouth moves, but nothing comes out.

He smiles. "Hi, sorry, but I just wanted to let you know…." He leans toward me, and it is right then that I realize he's the one wearing the cologne. He whispers near my ear, "You have, um… a bra…hanging off your pant leg."

"What?" I look down and…*OH MY GOD!*

There's a bra.

Hanging off my pant leg.

I reach down fast, swipe it up and shove it into my jacket pocket. Humiliating thoughts instantly fill my brain: I just walked through the mall this way! Trailing a bra! That I shoplifted! And this guy, of all people, saw it!

It brings me right back to an assembly fiasco I had in sixth grade, but this time I recover more quickly. At least there aren't a thousand eyeballs staring at me.

He laughs. Yes, laughs, and I want to drown myself in espresso.

"That happened to me once," he says, and I stare at him, imagining my face twenty shades of crimson. "Well, not with a bra," he adds fast, "but with a sock. Clinging from the dryer, I guess. I walked around school half the day that way until my buddy filled me in. S-o-o embarrassing."

I don't know whether to be glad he's sharing this or to still be mortified because a bra is *so* much worse than a sock. I get a better look at him now, while trying not to meet his eyes. He's taller than I am. His shoulders are broad. Did I mention he's really cute?

He holds his hand out for me to shake. "Hayden."

Hayden. "Hey," I say, shaking his hand. My heart's protesting and about to leap from my body. "I'm Claire."

"Hey, Claire," he says with a smile. "So…do you always walk around with a bra clinging to your pants?"

I crack up. "No," I say. "Not usually. Usually I drag a thong around."

I'm proud of myself for that new-found wit, and we both laugh.

"You're next," he says.

I stop laughing. "Huh?"

He smiles and points toward the counter. "It's your turn to order."

"Oh!"

I excuse myself, tripping over my own two feet. *Ugh, get a handle on yourself, Claire!* I place my order and pay for my mocha latte. While he orders his, I wait at another counter. I'm not sure what I should do when he comes over to wait for his coffee, too. Was he just being friendly before and that's that? Will he stand here awkwardly until he gets his coffee and then leave? Or will he try to talk to me some more? I take out my phone and pretend to check my texts.

"We meet again," he jokes.

"We do."

"Come here often?"

This makes me laugh again.

My name's called. I take my cup and thank the barista. There's a condiment station to my left, and I want to stall for time, so I pretend I need a few napkins, maybe an extra packet of sugar. I don't, but I add one anyway and then stir for a long minute.

His name's called next. I turn a little and peek through my eyelashes at him. He thanks the barista and hands her a tip. He's got blondish-brownish wavy hair that falls just past his ears, and his profile is handsome—a broad jaw with no facial hair and clear, smooth skin.

He comes over to me again. He's got gorgeous eyes and straight, white teeth. "So, where do you go to school?" he asks. "I go to JFK High."

I clear my throat. "Wellington."

"Cool. Sophomore?"

"How'd you know?"

He smiles and shrugs. "It's a gift."

I try to guess his grade, biting my lip and squinting my eyes. "Senior?" I ask.

"Yep."

"Cool. I'm gifted, too, it seems." There's a bit of awkward silence, so I sip my coffee again. "College plans?"

"No, actually. I'm into photography. I want to have my own business one day. What about you?"

"Well, my mom does hair. She's got a salon, and I work there sometimes. I think I'd like to be a stylist, too." He's nodding, like *yeah cool*, so I tell him photography is so boho and cool, too.

"So, are you here at the mall by yourself, or are you with someone?" he asks, then slaps himself in the forehead. "No, wait. That sounds terrible. I'm not asking because I'm a serial killer or anything."

That makes me laugh. *But wait. Would a serial killer actually say that? Or would they try to throw you off?* Mentally, I shake off the thoughts. *I've seen way too many episodes of* Zombified.

I compose myself. "I came to get boots. You?"

"I already have boots," he says, and when he smiles again, I relax. "I was actually here to meet someone who...kind of stood me up. Well, she did stand me up. Embarrassing." His face reddens.

"Oh, sorry." I pry my eyes from his. Who would be dumb enough to stand him up?

"It's all good," he says with a wave of his free hand. "She never answered my call, so it's not as if she stood me up. I mean, I didn't have to come here and wait for her."

"Yeah, but that still sucks," I say. "I'm sorry it didn't work out."

"It worked out."

He lifts his coffee cup as if to toast, and once I get that he means meeting me, I lift mine and we tap cups.

"Well, it was really nice to meet you," Hayden says after a sip. He points to my pocket, the one with the bra. "Thanks for the laughs."

"You too," I say my face burning up again. *You too? Can I sound any dumber?*

"Hey, um," he says, "I work over at The Photo Shoot, you know, the family portrait studio? I'm there after school on Mondays, Wednesdays and Fridays from 4 'til closing. If you're ever in the mall, and want a cup of coffee...I get a dinner break. If you want. To have coffee with me, I meant. Or dinner." He slaps his forehead again. It's adorable.

I smile.

"Sorry. I'm usually totally smooth with girls. *Not*."

All I can think of right now is how utterly cute his blotchy red cheeks are.

Stop it, stop it, stop it, Cupid! I feel something brush the back of my thigh. I check my butt for an arrow sticking out of it.

"You okay?" Hayden asks, looking behind me, too.

"Oh, yeah I was just…checking something."

"Checking for more hitchhiking bras?" he says.

I giggle. "Something like that."

"Can I give you my number?"

"Sure." I fish out my cell and open my contacts page. I type in his number and then type 'Hayden' in the spot for the name despite that my brain is firing off warning shots with flares: *Don't! You don't want a boyfriend! It doesn't matter if he's cute! Run!*

"Call if you want to get together okay?" he says.

I smile. "Okay."

So much for that.

"Well, bye, Claire. I hope to see you again soon."

As I watch him leave, I stand there, a smile frozen on my face. I want so desperately to call out, "No! I can't see you again! I meant what I said to Liv! No more dating!" But all that comes out next is, "Can't wait!"

You're so stupid, Cupid.

CHAPTER SIX

WAIT A MINUTE. Even if I want to, I can't call Hayden from my cell phone. He'll recognize it being the number he called, thinking it was that other girl. *If* I ever call him, that is. But maybe I should do something. Just in case I do need to call him.

It's possible. I mean, what if I needed to have my photo taken? I'd need his advice beforehand, wouldn't I? Sure, because I don't know anyone else in the photography business. And what if I wanted to know the difference between a photo and a portrait? Or what if I wanted to know what was better: candid shots or posed?

It's possible. Don't judge.

Anyway, it's always good to know people in different fields. It's called networking. You never know when you might need to speak to someone about any given subject.

So, it's decided. But first, I have to return the bra. When I go back into the store, the alarm goes off again. Now I know it went off before because of me.

"I took this by mistake," I tell the salesgirl when I take the bra out of my pocket and hand it to her. "It sort of…hitched a ride on my pants."

I leave the store, my face warm with embarrassment, as I head to the electronics store next. I want to buy a prepaid phone, one that can call and text and isn't expensive because I'll have to pay for it myself. The boots will have to wait.

When I get home, I program Hayden's contact info into the new phone and send him a quick test-text: **Hey, it's Claire.**

He answers seconds later: **Hey. :)**

Just wanted to give you my number.

Thanks. Hope to see you again.

Same :)

I lie on my bed and stare at the ceiling, thinking about Hayden…and the bra. My face warms all over again as I relive it, but this time I laugh at myself. I'm near hysterics thinking of how ridiculous that must've looked. Yet, Hayden was so cute about it. He totally didn't make me feel stupid. He *so* could have.

Maybe I'll show up at the mall one of these days, and Hayden and I can chat over a couple of lattes. Or even a slice of pizza. Yeah, nothing wrong with that. Just two people having a nice conversation, probably about photography and maybe having some innocent getting-to-know-each-other small-talk. As friends. Nothing serious. Because serious gets complicated.

Serious gets you a boyfriend, which gets you into trouble.

Serious is love. And I do *not* want that.

ON WEDNESDAY MORNING, I come downstairs for breakfast. I'm still thinking about meeting Hayden yesterday and how cute he is.

"Morning," I say to Mom who's standing at the stove, cooking eggs, totally oblivious and humming. It's only 6:13. How can anyone be so chipper in the morning?

"Morning, honey."

I reach for a box of cereal from the pantry.

"Claire, did you find boots?" Mom asks as she brings two

dishes of scrambled eggs to the table, where Evan is sitting, and places one in front of him.

"No," I say. "It was a bust." That word makes me think about bras again, and I laugh.

Mom's brows go up. "What's so funny?"

I wave my hand. "Oh, nothing, I was thinking about something I saw on TV last night."

Mom shrugs and gets up for some orange juice. "Teens…."

I lean over toward Evan. "Good luck with Leah at school today," I whisper.

Evan shoots me a dark look. "Shh!" He glances nervously toward Mom.

I lean in closer to him. "She didn't hear me," I whisper.

"Still…shh!"

Just then, Dad sweeps into the kitchen and kisses the back of Mom's head. "Morning, sweetie," he chirps. To Evan and me, he says, "Morning, you two."

"Good morning," Evan and I answer, but my words sound more like *"mmpff-pph"* because I'm chomping on a mouthful of cereal.

Soon we're all sitting around the table. Dad's talking about real estate (what else is new) and what leads he's following up on today, hoping to sell the Landry Estate. "That one," he says, popping a piece of bacon into his mouth, "will put me on the map *and* assist us in our Project-Get-Out-of-Debt cause." He winks at Mom, and she winks back.

I bring my bowl to the sink and rinse it. Then I kiss Mom and Dad goodbye.

"Good luck," I mouth to Evan whose eyes shift from Mom to Dad to make sure they didn't see that.

"Do you need a ride or are you taking the bus today, Claire-Bear?" Dad asks. I don't mind that he still calls me that, but he's the only one who's allowed to. It's better than all the stupid nicknames Evan used to tease me with: Claire-voyant, Claire-ity, and my personal favorite, his impression of the killer-maniac in *The Silence of the Lambs* saying "Hello, *Claire-iiice*." Not only is that creepy and weird because he loves all those ancient, classic movies, (thanks for introducing them to him, Dad) but I hate my real name.

"I'm going to bus it today, Dad, thanks," I say.

Since my breakup with Josh, Dad's been driving me every day so I don't have to see Briana on the bus. I can walk because it's not that far, but it's been so cold out, so I save that for better weather. Briana only lives about two blocks away, so we've shared a bus for forever. But I recently found out she's been getting a ride from her older brother and Josh always walks to school no matter the weather, so I don't have to worry about him.

When I get to school, my morning goes routinely with the exception that today, as well as all this past weekend, I'm thinking about Hayden. *Hayden, Hayden, Hayden.* I can't get him out of my head no matter how hard I try, especially during biology while Mr. Webber is rambling on about the life of a gypsy moth.

I start doodling Hayden's name over and over at the top of a blank page in my notebook, with a fancy capital H. Liv leans across our lab table, and before I can cover what I've written with my hand, her eyes almost look heart-shaped. "Who's Hayden?" she whispers, and then she waggles her eyebrows.

I cover the paper with my free hand. "No one," I whisper back. "I'm just doodling."

"Uh huh," she says, clearly unbelieving.

"Ms. Parker?" asks Mr. Webber. I look up, fast. "Is there something you need?"

"Sorry. No."

All eyes are staring at me. I feel it. Once again, I'm brought back to that sixth-grade assembly. I was supposed to give a simple speech, but I froze, and everyone suddenly fell silent. Until the laughter came. I stood there opening and closing my mouth, but words wouldn't come out. Finally, I ran off the stage, humiliated.

I stare at my paper now, willing myself to disappear or for Mr. Webber to focus on someone else. He doesn't.

"What's the answer?" Mr. Webber asks.

I haven't heard the question. My palms sweat. My upper lip does too, as the room grows more silent. Eyes are boring into my skin. I have nowhere to hide.

"Claire?"

I stand up fast and grab my things. "I—I need to go to the bathroom!"

"T.M.I.!" someone says, which causes a burst of laughter all around. Just like the assembly.

"Oh-*kaay*," Mr. Webber says, among giggles from the class. "Then I suppose you'll need a hall pass."

Before I can humiliate myself even more, I grab all my things including the pass from Mr. Webber, and rush out of the classroom. I head straight to the girls' bathroom in the art wing, passing a Cupid-gram guy on the way. He smiles at me, holding a bow and arrow, probably cardboard, which is covered in tinfoil, and his toga billows behind him as he walks. I nod fast and look away. Once he passes, I turn to see him going into my biology class. Perfect timing! I'm so glad he'll bring new attention to the class, and off of me.

Once I get to the girls' room, I lock myself in one of the stalls. I remain here for the rest of the period. As the late bell rings, Liv texts and tells me she got the Cupid-gram just now, and that I'd missed it. It was anonymous, she says, but she thinks it's this kid Andy.

At lunch, I'm back in the girls' room eating my banana and peanut-butter sandwich, leaning against the closed stall door. At least it's private. And no one's asking who Hayden is.

English is the last class of the day. It's my favorite class of them all. The only drawback is that Briana's in it.

I sit in the back of the class, which I prefer whenever possible because I have the view of the entire room (and the back of Briana's head, not her stupid face) and if I want, I can zone out. Up front, Ms. Levine writes details of the Shakespeare play we're reading, *A Midsummer Night's Dream,* on the smart board. She's writing out a list of themes related to this play, and we're supposed to pick one to write about in an essay, which will be due next Friday.

I consider the obvious theme: Love is Blind. I can go on and on about Titania and Bottom, whose head became a donkey's after a spell was cast on him by a trouble-making fairy named Robin Goodfellow, a.k.a. Puck. The spell placed on Titania was to make her fall in love with the first creature she saw when she woke from napping in the forest. This was all her husband's idea because he wanted something from Titania, which she refused to give him, so I guess he thought he could divert her attention.

Talk about manipulation.

But the more I think about it, the more I want to write about the character of poor Helena. I doubt Shakespeare considered it important, but Helena had some serious self-esteem issues. She loved Demetrius, but Demetrius loved Hermia, Helena's best friend. Helena lived in Hermia's shadow and always spoke about how Hermia was more beautiful, more interesting, more every-thing, than she was. And even when there was another spell placed on Demetrius to make him love Helena, and also after one was accidentally placed on Hermia's boyfriend which caused him to fall in love with Helena at the same time, Helena didn't believe any of it was true. She thought they were all making fun of her. She was always putting herself down.

I can totally relate to the whole 'loving someone who loves someone else' thing so I know how she must've felt. If she were a real person, I might help her think of ways to get revenge on them all for hurting her.

I'm chewing on the end of my pen, thinking of how to begin

my essay, while Ms. Levine gushes on and on about Shake-spearean greatness, when a folded note bops me in the head. I look up and see a kid whose name I don't know looking at me and smiling.

Carefully, so Ms. Levine doesn't hear the un-wrinkling of the paper, I open it. It says, "Can we talk?"

I look up again. He's still looking at me over his shoulder with a big, toothy grin.

I scribble a "?" on the note, fold it back up and toss it back to him. He reads it, writes again, and then sends the note back to me.

"I'm Andy," it says. "Can we talk at lunch?"

Andy? As in the Andy who possibly sent Liv a Cupid-gram?

I'm stunned for a moment and not sure what's going on. Like, seriously, *what the heck?*

"Claire?"

I look up and crumple the note in my palm. "Yeah?"

Ms. Levine is glaring at me. "I asked you a question."

Voices around me giggle. *Oh, no, not again.*

"Can you, um, repeat the question?" My skin gets hot and clammy. Just then, Briana looks back at me. *Is that a smirk?*

Ms. Levine sighs. "Where did Lysander and Hermia plan to marry?"

"Oh. I. Uh…" I wish this day was over.

Hands shoot up. Andy is mouthing the answer to me, but I can't make out what he's saying. Ms. Levine rolls her eyes and then calls on Briana.

"At Lysander's aunt's house, in the forest," Briana says. "Because she lived alone with no children and no one would find them there, especially Hermia's father, who forbade her to marry Lysander."

I roll my eyes.

"Excellent, Briana," Ms. Levine says before she gives me a dirty look and turns back to the whiteboard. Andy's turned back around, but I can't help wondering what that note was all about. I'll ask him after class. In the meantime, I'm trying to concentrate on not failing.

I honestly think that Shakespeare had at least one thing right —love makes people act ridiculously and unreasonably. I mean, even without Puck, who was always intervening, the characters in this play acted all messed up toward one another. Helena had every right to feel jealous when Demetrius caught sight of her best friend. The way he treated her was terrible! And though Helena got Demetrius's love in the end, it was really because of the reverse spell Puck put on him.

I wish I could change the ending of that play. I don't think that would go over very well though. But there's one thing I can do: change the ending of my own story. I need to figure out how not to be another Helena.

Back to this kid Andy. What's up with that? He sends Liv a Cupid-gram and then flirts with *me*? What nerve. Maybe instead of writing about Helena's insecurities, I should change my theme to: *Like All Guys, Love Stinks!*

CHAPTER SEVEN

AFTER ENGLISH, I wait until Briana leaves before I get up. I don't want to look at her conceited, smug face. I gather my books, but before I get to the doorway, Ms. Levine stops me.

"Is everything okay, Claire?" she asks. At least now the annoyed look is off her face. Now she seems concerned.

"Yes, thank you. I'm sorry about before. I wasn't paying attention. But I've read the play and plan to start my essay soon. I already know what theme I'm using."

"Well, that's good to hear," she says. "I'm worried about you. You seem distracted lately. Is it Briana?"

Ouch. I guess the entire school knows what happened. It was sort of a scandal. How could it not have been? Briana was one of my best friends, and Josh and I were together for almost a year.

"I was distracted, but I'm better now," I say and hope she can't tell that inside, I'm a big, fat mess. "I'll be more present tomorrow. Promise." I smile widely to show that I mean it.

She studies me a moment and then nods. "Okay. If you ever need to talk about anything, I'm here. I don't want your grades slipping."

"I appreciate that, but really, I'm fine. And they won't." My thumb pushes the button on the pen I'm holding in one hand, up and down, up and down. She looks at it, so I stop.

She smiles and nods. "Go before you miss your bus."

I thank her and leave, happy not to be in any more trouble. That's the last thing I need. As I come out of the room, I make a sharp right turn—and slam right into Andy.

"Hey, Claire. I hope you didn't get into trouble because of me."

"No, it's fine." We walk down the hall together in awkward silence.

"Oh, good. So, how's Liv?"

"She's okay." I have no idea why he's asking me about her.

"She's really nice," he says. He's kind of cute. I never noticed that before.

"She's the best," I say and make my way through the maze of people in the hall. I'm about to ask about his note, but as we reach my locker, Liv approaches.

"See ya, Claire," Andy says suddenly and disappears down the hall.

"That was weird," I say opening my locker and pulling one of my notebooks out.

"Since when do you talk to Andy?" Liv asks.

"I don't. He passed me a note in class just now. He asked if we could talk. Then he acted strange when he saw you just now."

Liv frowns. "He wants to talk to you? About what?"

"I don't know. Are you sure he could have sent the Cupid-gram? It really could've been anyone. Hashtag truth."

"I know, but...I think it was him. I can tell. The way I catch him looking at me sometimes."

I shut my locker door and face her, smiling. "You like him, don't you?"

"Me? No. Maybe. Yeah." She smiles, too.

"I knew it! You should get together with him then."

Her smile fades. "Not if he likes you."

"He doesn't like me," I say fast, hoping it's true. Maybe I misread things.

Her face lights with an idea. "You should go to the dance with him. He's cute, sweet, and I love the edgy way he dresses." What that's got to do with anything, I don't know, but I do agree, he knows how to dress. Today he wore a silver chain that went from the front of his black jeans to the back pocket, and a simple white t-shirt under a red-checkered flannel.

"I mean, he'd be perfect to send Josh the message that you're over him, just because of how cool Andy is. Plus, you can ask him about me."

"Ah, I knew there'd be another reason. Although, I like how you think, Liv." *Like me.*

She laughs. "Just think about it," she says. "Because I heard that Josh and Briana are definitely going to be there."

"Awesome." We begin to walk down the hall, and I fill her in about Briana upstaging me in English.

Liv rolls her eyes. "She's changed so much. Who *is* she lately?"

"I don't know either."

When we get to the exit doors, Liv says, "So what happened to you in bio before? Was it the assembly thing again?"

She knows me so well. "Yeah, sorry. I wasn't paying attention, and when everyone looked at me, it kind of freaked me out."

Liv gives me a sympathetic look, complete with a pouty lip. She's such a good friend. I should tell her about Hayden and the mall. I know she'd be upset if she found out another way and not from me. But on the other hand, she'll never let it go if I do tell her now. She'll be all over it, insisting I give it a fair chance and pushing me to date Hayden, a guy I barely know. I decide to keep things to myself for now.

And what if Andy asks me out? Even though I've never done anything to make him think I like him, it would be awful if he did. It would totally upset Liv. She's such a good friend to me. She doesn't deserve that.

Ugh. Why is everything getting so complicated? I'm beginning to feel like *I'm* living in *A Midsummer Night's Dream.*

CHAPTER EIGHT

ALL THE WAY HOME, I stew over Briana and all she's done to me. I really wish she wasn't in any of my classes. Her upstaging me today has really got me in a crappy, sappy mood. So much so that when I get home, I fish out the picture of Josh and me, the one that was taken at his parents' beach house last June where we spent an entire day. It's a selfie he took of us with the ocean in the background. His arm is around my shoulder, our temples are touching, and we're smiling. We were so happy.

But were we? My mind wanders back to that day. After dinner, we'd walked the boardwalk that paralleled the beach. At first everything was fine. But then someone came up to him. A girl. And she was really pretty. They hugged, and Josh introduced me to her.

I waved hi, and she did too, and she seemed nice enough, but was that smile and the look she gave him too much? And then that hug? And the way she giggled a little too much when he said something that wasn't even that funny? As they spoke, trying but failing to include me, thoughts invaded my mind. Thoughts like: *he likes her. He's going to dump me and go out with her. She's so pretty. Stop it; she's just a friend. But look at how he's gazing at her!*

They said goodbye and I was so mad that I couldn't speak. Josh kept asking me what was wrong. The most I could muster in answer was a mumbled, "Nothing," until we got to the beach. We walked a few feet in the sand, and I couldn't take it anymore, so I asked him who she was.

"We've been friends forever," he said. I waited, so he said it again: "*Friends*, Claire."

I crossed my arms over my chest and played with the promise ring Josh had given me: a silver faux sapphire shaped like a heart with two rhinestone chips on each side. "Looked like more than just friends to me. Did you see how she looked at you?"

"Listen. I'm with you. Not her. Or anyone else." He kissed my forehead, then the tip of my nose, then my lips. I calmed down and let it go, but we argued about another girl not long after that. Then Briana happened. So I was right.

Yes, I was right.

The picture looks blurry now through my stupid tears. Why am I giving Josh—or Briana—this much power over me? It's time to put it away for good, along with everything else he ever gave me or reminds me of him. I find a shoebox in my closet and pluck things one by one to stash inside of it: the Cupid card, a few pictures, letters he wrote to me during study hall one day after I'd told him I thought it would be so romantic to read hand-written notes instead of texts, and a pair of silver heart-shaped stud earrings.

I close the box and jam it up onto the top shelf in the closet.

This is why I don't want another boyfriend. It hurts way too much. As cute as Hayden is and as sweet as he seemed, I know I shouldn't call him and chance seeing him anymore. What if we become fast friends and then I fall for him? And then, what if we have a relationship and I find out he's a cheater, too? And what was I thinking getting a whole new phone just to text and call him? I've made things way too complicated, and I know I'm totally overthinking things, which is making everything even more confusing.

I have to be honest and tell him what happened, about the mistaken phone call and how it was all a misunderstanding. Maybe he'll be okay with it, and we'll be friends. Just friends. Nothing more. Maybe one day we *can* be more. When I'm ready. Or never. Besides, he's probably going to call me a big jerk and hang up on me once I tell him what happened.

Either way, I have to face the music.

I reach for my cell phone, but before I call him, I rehearse what I think I should say out loud as I pace my room:

"Hey, listen, I got your call by mistake, and then, instead of calling you right back to let you know you had the wrong number, I stalked you at the mall and then pretended to have a chance meeting with you at the coffee shop after you spotted a bra on my pants."

God, no. Maybe I'll just text him. That's easier and less embarrassing.

I type fast, my thumbs going a mile a minute across the touch-screen keyboard:

Hey! So this is Claire, the girl you met yesterday at Star-bucks, not the girl you met at that party. You called me by mistake, but it's okay because I came to the mall anyway and we seemed to have hit it off after you pointed out the bra on my leg.

UGH! I erase that and try a joking approach next:

Hey, funny thing happened—you got the wrong number and got me (Claire) by mistake. So I went to the mall to check you out (no, I'm not a deranged stalker, but I did think you were a serial killer! Ha!)...

OMG, no.

Finally, I settle on:

Hey.

I think that once we begin talking, things may come out

organically. I send it fast, and my heart is leaping in my chest while I wait for a response. Finally, my phone chimes, and I rush to open the message. It's him.

Hey, April. I didn't think I'd hear back from you. :)

April? Who's April?

Then it hits me. I used the wrong phone! Now he thinks I'm the other girl, the one he originally called. I am so stupid.

Before I can respond or figure out what to do, he writes: **I'm glad you texted. :)**

Wait. He's glad?

Still there? he says.

I think fast and play along: **Yeah. Just wanted to say I'm sorry for not calling you back.**

I can tell he's typing by the three dots. Then they disappear. Then reappear. Finally, they disappear for a few moments. Is he nervous? Maybe I'm jumping to conclusions.

I reread what we've written so far. It could be that he's being nice to her. I think I need to be honest here. I don't even know this guy, and I'm meddling in his life. It's not right. And maybe if this April chick was blowing him off and being super mean by giving him the wrong number, he deserves to hear something positive. I have the power to do that right now, so I think I will. That way, he can move on without feeling like total crud.

I begin to type: **But I'm writing to let you know that I have a boyfriend and I'm sorry I didn't tell you when we met, but I got all caught up in the moment and then my phone broke and—**

I don't get to send it because Hayden sends another text before I can finish:

That's okay. You've been on my mind since we met.

So he does like her. And here I am trying to make him feel better.

A couple of moments later, another text comes through. **I've been wanting to talk to you.**

Here it comes. He's going to ask her out because he thinks she's hot. Guys can be so predictable sometimes.

You deserve someone who will treat you better than your ex did.

So she has an ex and he wants to be her Prince Charming now? Take advantage of her vulnerability? Gross.

My fingers hover over the keys. I'm not sure what to say, although I've got a lot of choice words on the tip of my tongue—or my fingers. In the end, though, I decide I'm going to let this April chick end things with Hayden right now:

Thanks but I'm not ready to be in another relationship right now. I hit send.

:(

Really? A sad face? That's it! I'm telling him to shove off in every way possible: **You're a jerk! Eff off! See ya!** I'm typing the words when his next text stops me dead.

I actually just met someone.

My heart lurches in my chest. *Does he mean me? And is he telling her so she thinks he doesn't care because she just blew him off?*

Cool, I write back.

I'm frozen, thinking of what to say next when Evan opens my door a crack and peeks in. I shove the phone under my pillow.

"Ever hear of knocking?" I say.

"Sorry. I forgot."

"Ugh. Don't do that again."

"I won't." Evan's face lights up. "I asked Leah out today."

Mine brightens. "And?"

"She said yes."

"Cool! What did you say? What did she say?"

"I said hi, she said hi back. Then I made a joke about something our French teacher said today, and she laughed."

"She laughed? See, I told you so."

"Yeah. Then I asked if she wanted to hang out one day after school, and she said sure."

"Awesome." The buzzing of another text alert drives me nuts. I have to see what Hayden's saying. But first, I need to make sure Evan knows the deal. "Just be cautious," I tell him.

"Why? What's she going to do?"

I shrug. "All I'm saying is you should be careful. Don't be too trusting. People cheat."

"Do you think she will? Cheat on me?"

"Anything's possible. Don't be naïve."

For the next five minutes, I'm explaining what naïve means, and all the while, Hayden's texting. Finally, Evan understands.

"I'll be careful," he says. "So can you maybe ride with us to the mall one afternoon next week? Mom won't let me go on the bus without you."

More buzzing. "Yeah, sure."

"'K. Thanks."

"No problem."

Evan finally disappears and closes my door. I read the two new texts: **Yeah, it is cool. We seemed to hit it off.** Then, **I hope she calls me**.

It feels like there's a swarm of hornets in my belly. He seems serious, but how can I tell he's not just playing hard to get? Relationships are always so complicated. On one hand, I already feel giddy and shaky inside whenever I think of him, and I don't even know him! And why do I care about him liking someone else? On the other hand, he's acting like a typical guy. A cheat and a liar. Like Josh.

From the corner of my eye, I spot something on the floor by my closet. It's the old Valentine's Day card from Josh. I was sure it was in the box before I put it away. It must have dropped out.

I sneer at the Cupid on the cover. Then I fall back on my pillow and cover my face with both hands.

"Go away, Cupid," I say into them. "Go bother someone else!"

CHAPTER NINE

THE NEXT MORNING when I come downstairs for breakfast, Mom and Dad are already at the table, eating bagels with cream cheese. Their coats are draped over their chairs because they'll leave right after Evan and I do. Speaking of Evan, he walks in behind me. Whistling.

I turn to him. He waggles his eyebrows. I think there's a skip in his step.

"Morning," Mom says. Dad looks up and gives me a nod.

"Morning," I say.

Evan's still smiling. He looks like a lovesick maniac. He grabs a bagel and sits at the table.

Dad chuckles. "Somebody's happy," he says in Evan's direction. Then he pats the empty seat beside him. "Come and sit with us, Claire Bear."

Even if I was starving, I couldn't deal with his mood right now. Too much happy coming from Evan. Don't get me wrong, I'm happy things are starting to go well with Leah, but it just feels a little salt-in-the-wound to me right now. Plus, Josh and Hayden are wrestling in my head. I try to push both of their faces out of my brain and think of something else—anything: the space shuttle on TV last night, Gran's awesome triple-chocolate brownies, the cat Liv told me she wants to adopt from a shelter—but it's no use.

I grab an apple out of the bowl on the counter and kiss my parents goodbye. I'm walking today, so I have to go now in order to be on time. It's not that far to school, and I like the walk sometimes. I pull my coat on along with my backpack, and as I step into the brisk morning air, my new phone buzzes. It's Hayden.

Morning

Morning! Maybe I shouldn't have added the exclamation point. It was probably too much.

Are you busy tomorrow night?

I decide to be completely cautious. **Not sure yet. Why?** I'm walking and thinking, my feet scraping the sidewalk. I get to the corner and cross the street.

He sends another message: **Zombie Apocalypse is playing. Love zombies. :) Corny, I know.**

I nearly walk into a tree. I right myself and write back fast: **So not corny! I love zombies. *Zombified's* my fave show ever!**

Mine too! Did you see last episode?

Of course!

How awesome was it when The Zombie Master ordered the Level 5-ers to attack the coroner and then they feasted on the bodies?

IKR?!

Epic!

We talk more zombie stuff until I get to school, which happens way too quickly.

So, movies?

My stomach flips. **Sure.**

Dinner first?

Okay :)

Awesome. TTYL

I shove my phone back into my purse. I'm so deep in thought

about how cool it is that Hayden's into zombies that I don't realize I just said yes to a date.

HAYDEN PICKS me up at 5:30 Friday night. Mom asks a thousand questions, like she's in the CIA, the FBI, and even the IRS. *Finally*, after all questions are answered, Hayden takes me to a Chinese restaurant. It's so pretty with hanging lanterns and soft lighting. Immediately, my stomach rumbles when I walk in. It smells like Chinatown in New York. I remember vividly when Mom and Dad took Evan and me one year. We go to sit down, and Hayden pulls my chair out. Then he orders two sodas.

We look over the menu, and I decide on sesame chicken, my favorite. He asks for shrimp lo mein with fried rice.

The server brings our sodas. We talk while we wait for the food to arrive, mostly about school and a little about our families, but after a minute, I have to say what I'm thinking.

"I'm really sorry if I come off looking like a freak sometimes." I swirl the ice in my cup with the straw. "This stupid upcoming school dance must be getting to my head."

"A freak?" Hayden looks confused.

I sigh and begin again. "It's just that…I'm being careful about relationships. I wasn't exactly treated well by my ex. I guess I'm still bitter." I think about how one month ago, I was so sad I could hardly speak.

"I get that. I've had my share of breakups," he says. "Well, one. But it was messy."

I didn't even consider that he could've had a similar experience to mine.

Hayden takes my hand and leans over our table. His hand is warm, gentle. He's got the most perfect jawline. And those chiseled cheek bones. And his eyes….

"I like you, Claire. You're pretty and funny and fun to be

around. So if we're just friends, I guess that's fine. Maybe one day it can be more."

I melt. Right into my chair.

He squeezes my hand. "But that doesn't mean I'm not willing to wait for you to be ready. If, you know, you like me, too. Do you?"

I swallow hard. Blink. I'm battling in my head, fighting to stay faithful to myself, to not be vulnerable ever again. But there's another side that's winning—the side that *does* like him.

"I'm sorry," he says. "You don't have to answer that. I guess I'm eager. I've always been an over-achiever. Hey, and I'm a poet. Wait for iiiit…."

At the same time, we say, "And I know it."

We laugh at that, and though I'm smiling on the outside, on the inside, I'm tangled up in emotions. I'm glad, confused, giddy, and more terrified than ever.

"Excuse me," the server says, and she places our plates in front of us.

I snap to. "Sorry. Thank you."

"Your face is red," he says.

My hands find my cheeks. "Ugh! It happens a lot."

"I think it's adorable." He sips his Coke, his eyes still on me. "So what's this dance you were telling me about?"

"Oh, that." I wave my hand. "It's just a lame winter dance called The Cupid Connection. Dumb. And it's on Valentine's Day."

"Seems appropriate."

"It is, but I'm not fond of Valentine's Day."

"How come?"

"Let's just say the last good one I had was when my dad gave me a heart-shaped box of chocolates when I was nine."

"Well, you need to have a better Valentine's Day. Maybe you will this year."

I get chills up and down my arms. Can I even imagine that

with him? I swipe the thought away as we pick up our chopsticks and begin to eat.

"Or maybe," he says between chews, "maybe we should make up our own holiday, an entirely new one to replace it. How about...Finding a New Love Day?"

"That's kind of long. I don't think it'll fit on a card."

"You have a point. What about just New Love Day?"

"Hmm. I like the sound of that."

"Me too. So that's what we'll celebrate this year. New Love Day."

We eat for a few minutes. I'm about to ask about the movie when he asks, "Are you going with someone? To the dance?"

"Sort of. I'm going with Liv."

"Will your ex be there?" he asks.

The mention of Josh, even if he didn't use his actual name, shocks me. I place my chopsticks down and wipe my chin with my napkin.

"Sorry. I shouldn't have asked you that."

"It's okay. He'll be there. But he's with someone new. My ex-best friend."

Hayden winces. I look at my plate.

"I've been hurt myself," he says. "My ex and I were dating for about a year. She cheated."

I look up.

"It hurt," he says. "You get that though, huh?"

"Yeah."

"I got over her, but not the feeling of being lied to. I can't ever go through that again. Know what I mean?"

"Yep," is all I can say, but on the inside, I'm screaming at myself to come clean with him right now. To tell him everything because he's being so open with me and he seems genuine and sweet and neither of us wants to get hurt again. I want to tell him how he called me by accident, that our "chance" meeting wasn't by chance, not entirely, and how I've been pretending to be April. If I tell him now, it won't be as bad as waiting. I have to tell him.

"Hayden, I have to tell you—"

"You know, Claire," he interrupts. "That's what I like about you. You're real. You've got this *take me as I am* attitude. The real deal."

Gulp.

Hayden looks at his cell phone. "We should finish up. The movie starts in half an hour."

We finish eating, and when we're done, Hayden walks me to the car and opens the door. When he comes around to the driver's side, he buckles up and looks over at me. "What was it you wanted to say before? I think I cut you off."

"Oh, I don't even remember," I say. How can I say what I wanted now that he told me how real I seem to him and how he can't deal with a liar? That's what I am. A liar.

"Wasn't important then," he jokes and starts the engine. "Ready to go?"

"I'm always ready for zombies."

Once inside the movie theater, Hayden's hand brushes against mine as we walk. His arm hairs tickle my skin. A strange feeling washes over me, and I suddenly get the urge to grab his hand in mine. Could I be that bold? If I don't ever talk to him again as April and if I forget about telling him how he called me randomly that first time, *can* we have a relationship that's not based on lies? If we start from today and move forward? New Love Day?

"Popcorn?" he asks, pointing to the candy counter with his thumb. "I don't think they have mocha lattes."

I giggle. "That's okay. I'm not that addicted to caffeine. Even though I'd love one."

"Then we'll have to go out again soon. We'll get mocha lattes —three pumps of chocolate in yours."

I stop and study him. "How did you—"

"I pay attention." He steps closer to me. There's this magnetic force field pulling me in closer...closer.

And right in the middle of the movie theater lobby, Hayden kisses me.

On the cheek.

Dang it.

Okay, I know I said that I wanted to take things slowly, but I bet even Cupid would agree—a girl can change her mind.

CHAPTER TEN

I CAN'T GET Hayden's face out of my head all weekend, no matter how hard I try. I see it when I close my eyes, when I look in the fridge for a snack, and even when I'm scrolling social media.

I'm thinking about him on Monday too, while Liv's talking about the decorations as we walk to class. She's saying how The Cupid Connection dance will be *soo* awesome. I hear her speaking, but all I can think about is the way Hayden held the door. The way he held my hand. How he put his arm around me during the movie and pulled me closer whenever it was scary. Most of all? I'm thinking about how he knows I take three pumps of chocolate in my mocha lattes.

I'm fighting the urge to vomit when she discusses the paper hearts we will be cutting out of red poster board to hang all over the gym. The queasy feeling gets worse when I see Josh and Briana down the hall. Briana's hanging all over him, and he's hanging all over her. Josh catches my eye and holds it.

How can he look at me while kissing her? Deliberately, I look the other way.

Liv tugs my sleeve. "Hey. You okay?" she says, but before I can answer her, Briana pulls away from Josh and looks over at me, like she's just figured out that her boyfriend is looking at something other than her own dumb face.

Liv follows my glare in their direction and scowls. After the Incident in December, Liv has always had my back. She knew that Briana was supposed to be my friend and that she'd hooked up with my boyfriend and that was wrong. Period.

Liv's right. Even if they seem happy together, much happier than Josh and I ever were, she still did wrong by me. Girl Code.

"Let's go," I say. "They're not worth it."

When we get to the bottom of the steps by the front office, out of Briana's sight, she says, "You okay now?"

She always knows. I take a slow, deep breath and blow it through my lips. "You know what? I am," I say. For the first time, I'm not a complete mess after seeing them. It feels good.

"Good," she says. "Because you're always going to see them. It's inevitable. You need a distraction. That's why I've been pushing you to meet other guys and go to the dance anyway. I don't mean to make you feel bad. You deserve to be happy, Claire."

I look at her, and I can tell she means it.

"Thanks, Liv. I'll think about it."

We continue walking to class through the thinning crowd. The warning bell is going to ring any second, so we quicken our steps. I want to tell her about Hayden, but it's not the right time yet. I want to be sure of things myself before I go and blab everything to her. If I tell her too soon, she'll be on me about it every millisecond. I'll have to wait a little while more.

When we reach the end of the hall there's a tap on my shoulder.

It's Briana.

"What do you want?" Liv says, squeezing into the space between Briana and me. I gently push her aside so I can see Briana's face.

"Relax, *Olivia*. I just want to talk to her," Briana says.

"She has nothing to say to you."

I look at Liv. "I can handle this myself," I say. Then to Briana, I say, "I have nothing to say to you."

"Well, then maybe you can just *listen*."

"Are you kidding?" Liv says her voice loud in the now-empty hall. "*Listen*? She doesn't want to hear *anything* you have to say!"

"Liv, I got this," I say, and then turn back to Briana. "I don't want to hear *anything* you have to say."

Briana huffs and then digs around in her purse. "Whatever." She pulls out some random items. "Josh wanted me to give these back to you. He was going to do it himself, but I was tired of waiting. So, here."

She can't meet my eyes as she hands me a keychain I gave him, black with a dangling shark tooth on it. After that, she hands me a John Mayer CD I gave him for his birthday. "Oh, and you left this at my house." She plops my Pearly Pink lip gloss into my hand along with a turquoise necklace my grandparents gave to me a gazillion years ago. I thought I'd lost it.

I stare at the things she placed into my hand. It hurts knowing we were once great friends. We knew each other's secrets. We slept at each other's houses. We were, all three of us, always together. But for her to give me stuff from Josh? That's so not right. I'm totally lost for words.

I'm so glad Liv's not. "Wow, Briana," Liv says. "Way to be a best friend."

She glares at Liv. "What was I supposed to do? Neither of you cared about me or cared about what I wanted." Her eyes are filling up. It almost makes me feel bad for her. Almost.

"What are you talking about?" I manage.

But before she can answer, one of the shop teachers appears and clears his throat. Shoot. The bell rang and the hallway is completely clear.

"Where do you ladies belong?"

My heart is in my throat. We all begin to stutter.

"Get to the front office for tardy slips before all three of you get detention."

We practically run from him. None of us says another word as I stuff the things into my purse.

At the front office, we're met with dirty looks from Ms. Lockheart, one of the secretaries. I can feel Liv's anger toward Briana, who is cowering beside me, after she's handed her slip.

"Get to class, girls," says Ms. Lockheart. "And don't let me see you back here again any time soon or you'll have a date with Mr. Hillman."

Mr. Hillman, the assistant principal, a.k.a. Mr. Hit-man.

We rush out of there, and after we're clear of mean secretaries and hitmen, I notice a strange look on Briana's face. Does she care how badly she hurt me? Why does she only seem to care about herself? My heart lurches a little, remembering how close we used to be. But then I remember Josh and it hardens again.

"Claire, I want to tell you how sorry—" she begins, but Liv holds up a hand.

"Don't go there," Liv tells her. "She doesn't need this right now, so back off."

Briana's about to say something else, but I interject. "Let's just get to class before we get into more trouble." If we stand here any longer, Liv might tell her how sad I've been. The last thing I want right now is Briana's sympathy. At the same time, I'm curious to know what she was about to tell me. Obviously, it was the beginning of an apology. But what could she possibly say? That she's sorry for stealing my boyfriend? How could I forgive that? And how dare Briana give me back those things, and how dare Josh make her do it and then her try to say she's sorry?

Let her have him. They deserve each other.

After school, in my room, I go straight to the box of Claire-and-Josh things and get to work ripping and tearing everything in it. Then I gather everything Briana ever gave me, too: photos, best-friend necklace, bracelets we made in eighth-grade summer camp, and toss every last bit of it into the trash.

Liv's been texting me since I got home. I send her a quick response, telling her I have a migraine. I hate to lie to her but I have to be alone. I'm not sure how to feel right now. On one hand, I'm pissed at Josh and Briana. On the other hand, do I really care as much as I once thought? *Am* I moving on? When I think of Hayden, his face replaces Josh's. I feel differently about him than Josh or any boy I've ever liked. Still, I'm not sure I can trust him either.

I decide to work on my English paper. Before I write, I think for a while about how Helena was timid, always feeling like a victim. She was totally untrusting. I wonder what could have made her feel so low about herself. Maybe she and Demetrius had a relationship going on and she totally trusted him but then he cheated on her.

He probably did. Maybe he cheated with Hermia. That had to be it. And then she literally chased Demetrius through the woods. Only after the love spell, he chased *her*. So did Lysander.

I think a while on this, too. What if Josh and Andy chased after me? It would have to be because of a love spell. Ordinarily, they'd both go after Liv. That's totally believable. She's just as gorgeous as Briana, if not more. But maybe they're both a little insecure, too.

Hermia was. She doubted herself at one point at the end of the play. Maybe confidence is the answer, even if you're faking it. Maybe Briana and Liv already do that. Maybe that's why Josh was attracted to Briana. She seemed confident.

Yes, that's it. I bet Helena might have won Demetrius over if she had been confident.

CHAPTER ELEVEN

I NEED to be more confident. Even though I don't want a boyfriend, having confidence will help me with other things in life, like grades and even giving speeches in front of a bazillion people. Maybe I can fake it.

After school on Tuesday, I get a text from Hayden, and my heart leaps in my chest. Except it's on my old phone, and it's to April, not me.

Hey, April. There's a party at Mark's on Saturday. After the game. Just wanted to let you know. Hope to see you there.

I don't answer. I can't. What is he doing, asking her out? After the movies on Friday, I thought he was different. Maybe just a little. At least enough to stand out from the rest. But no, I was right all along. I think back to the wish I made with Liv and announce a new one in my room for the Universe to hear loud and clear. "I wish there were honest, good guys left on the planet!"

Not that I want a boyfriend or anything.

I stare at the text. Read the words over and over. I knew it. He likes her. And the fact that I feel so badly about it means I'm falling for him.

Between this and Briana's baloney yesterday, I'm tempted to text Hayden and tell him I'm onto him, but Evan knocks on my door. "Claire?"

"Yeah?"

He opens the door a crack. "Mom and Dad are downstairs cooking dinner."

"Thanks for the newsflash. I'd be lost without that info."

"Anytime." Sarcasm is a Parker trait, like brown eyes or big feet. "Listen, can you still take Leah and me to the mall after school tomorrow?"

"I already said I would." I actually forgot. And now I'm wondering: Do I want to risk seeing Hayden? *Yes. I do.*

"Well, Mom wants me to confirm. She wants to talk to you about it." He rolls his eyes. "Sometimes I'm sorry I told them about her." I remember how it felt to be thirteen—not old enough to do most things alone and always having to rely on your parents for everything. Even though I have to ride my bike or take the bus to get places because my road test isn't for a few more months, at least I have more freedom than him.

And he wants to go to the mall. It must be a sign.

The phone buzzes in my hand. **Hey. What are you doing tomorrow? Come see me at work. Break at 5.**

I type fast without thinking. **Do you know who this is?**

Huh?

It's me, Claire.

He types, pauses, types again. Then: **I know it's you. ???**

Now my phone rings. "Yes, I'll take you," I tell Evan, shooing him out of my room. "And tell Mom I'll be right down."

I answer the call. "Hello." I say it like I'm annoyed and unamused. But really, my heart's pounding so hard I might pass out.

"Are you all right?" he asks.

"I'm fine."

"What did you mean before? Who else would I be talking to?"

Oh, this is so easy. I have to swallow the words down so they don't escape my mouth. I'll wait to see if he slips. Besides I can't show my hand in this poker game. He'd know I was posing as April.

"I just wanted to know if you knew, that's all," I say.

He chuckles, like he's nervous. "Okay."

There's a moment of silence until he clears his throat. "So will you come by tomorrow?"

I relax a bit. He's so nice to me. I'll give him another chance. Maybe he's just being friendly with April and nothing's going on between them. I think back on how I was often jealous of Josh talking to other girls. Maybe I *was* insecure. Maybe that had something to do with our breaking up. Like one-tenth of it.

"Sure. I'm taking my brother and his girlfriend to the mall anyway."

"Okay, great. See you tomorrow. Have fun at school."

"You too." We hang up and I'm staring at the phone. I have to go, or I'll be late. But I can't move. I'm so confused. He seems to like me. But then there's April. I need to know more about her.

I grab my other phone, and as April, I type: **Maybe.** I hit send fast before I change my mind. Instantly there's a reply: **Cool!**

How am I supposed to build my confidence when the guy I loved cheated, and now the guy I'm really starting to like, despite my not wanting a boyfriend, is double dealing? Why are all guys so awful? I'm not sure. But I *do* know that I'm not letting anyone hurt me ever again.

CHAPTER TWELVE

WEDNESDAY AFTER SCHOOL, I slip into my black jeans, a burgundy band t-shirt that my dad bought me, and my black-and-white checkered Vans with the white laces. I inspect myself in the stand-up mirror behind my bedroom door. "Ugh. Too corny." I pull my hair out of the pony tail, toss the t-shirt, and opt for a white button-down with a black collar. "Much better."

And why do I care what I look like? This isn't a date or anything. I'm just supervising Evan and Leah at the mall, and meeting a friend. That's it.

When I get to the kitchen to let Mom know we're about to leave for the bus, I walk in on a lovey-dovey groping session between her and Dad. Gross.

I clear my throat loudly. "A-hem. Hello? People in the room." I shield my eyes with my free hand as I reach for some OJ in the fridge and then a glass from above the sink.

Mom giggles, which makes it even creepier, and as I pour my juice, I have to erase visions of them making out from my head. It is their twentieth anniversary this weekend, so they're more lovey-dovey than usual, but *must we*? I mean, yeah, I get that they love each other after all these years, but I don't need to be reminded every ten minutes.

After a big swig of juice, I yell for Evan, hoping to just get out of here fast so I can change the scenery in my brain. "Let's go!"

"What about dinner?" Mom asks.

"I can buy them pizza at the mall. I'll fend for myself. Besides I'm not hungry. Had a big lunch," I lie. Truth is, I've got no appetite.

"Be home by nine, please," Mom says as Dad kisses her once more on her cheek.

"I'll pick you up at the bus stop tonight," Dad informs me, tapping an imaginary watch on his wrist. "Nine."

"Fine. 9:00. Got it."

"Can't it be 9:30?" Evan says, bursting into the room and pulling on his parka. "I don't want to seem too juvenile to Leah."

"You *are* juvenile," I tell him and get a dirty look in response, so I retort: "Well, why do you think I'm chaperoning you two?"

"Shut up."

"You have *such* a way with words," I say.

"Nine. Not a moment later," Mom repeats. "Make sure you get the 8:30 bus. And Claire, make sure they're in your sight the entire time in the mall. I don't want any panicked phone calls saying you've lost them."

"Got it. No losing Evan."

Another eye roll from Evan warrants one from me, too. I can't help it this time.

"Leah's getting dropped off there and will meet you, right?" Mom asks Evan.

Evan shrugs. "Yeah, sure. Whatever."

"No, not *whatever*." Mom looks serious now. "If she's getting dropped off, I hope whoever does the dropping waits for you two to get there before they leave."

Evan opens his mouth, but I intercept before his curfew is cut even more. "Mom, I'm sure Leah's family won't do a drive-by drop off." As Mom seems to consider this, I quickly add, "And I'll be sure to say hi before they leave and give them my cell number." I feel inside my purse, making sure I have both of my phones. I do.

"Good thinking, Claire Bear," Dad says.

Evan sighs hard. "I'm not a baby, you guys. I can take care of myself."

"Want me to call this whole thing off?" Mom says as I secretly give him the throat-slice sign. Evan takes the hint. He mumbles something under his breath, and then he stomps out of the kitchen toward the front door.

I shake my head and share an empathetic look with my parents. "Kids today...."

Mom smiles as Evan and I kiss her and Dad goodbye. Then we head out the door before more parental tyranny can occur.

The bus ride is shorter than usual today. Less stops, I guess. Once we're at the mall, I do what I said I would—say hi to Leah's mom, who did not do a drive-by drop off, and give her my cell phone number. Responsibilities behind me, I allow Evan and Leah to walk twenty paces ahead. "If you lose me," I say to Evan, "meet me at the food court at eight."

"Got it."

We stroll along, and I watch as he struggles with his hand behind Leah. I cringe for him, knowing how nervous he must be and how much he really wants to hold her hand. He tries and then chickens out. A moment later, he tries again before giving up and shoving his hand in his front jeans' pocket. She's talking a mile a minute and giggling though, so it seems she has no idea of Evan's dilemma. It's adorable. They're adorable together.

We head down the west wing and pass window after window of nicely dressed—although headless—mannequins. Two, a man and a woman, look as though they're having a conversation. Her arms are up; he's facing the other way. I picture the scene. She's telling him off for hurting her and he couldn't care less. Even mannequin guys are pigs.

As we approach Starbucks, I can smell the roasted coffee beans and hear the whooshing of the frothers as baristas make their drinks. My heart picks up and my stomach trembles as I recall meeting Hayden here the other day.

I've already lost sight of Evan and Leah. They've probably slipped into a store. I check around me and finally spot them in H&M. Leah's still talking and giggling while browsing the racks. From here, I can see Evan's crimson cheeks, as red as the Brick Red Crayola that comes in the crayon pack. I catch his eye and mouth: *Food court. 8:00,* while pointing to my wrist as if I'm wearing a watch, which I'm not. Evan gives me thumbs-up and is wearing this gigantic goofy grin that makes me laugh. I'm not sure if my laughing is coming from his face looking that hilarious, or if I'm a jiggly ball of nerves. In any case, I take a deep breath and make my way toward The Photo Shoot.

But with every step, I feel weaker, more jiggly. Now my ears burn and my throat is closing.

"It's just coffee," I tell myself again and wipe my sweaty hands on my pant legs.

When I get to The Photo Shoot, there are people in the waiting area, which is filled with red hearts hanging from the ceiling, pasted onto the counter, and the walls. It looks like Cupid threw up in here. Why does everyone make such a big deal out of Valentine's Day?

I look around for Hayden. There are customers and workers bustling around. Along the walls are portraits of perfect-looking families. One's of a couple lying on a grassy field. The man is on his back, the woman lying on her side, gazing lovingly down at him. *More sappy love garbage.*

Someone's number is called, and I see a woman and her three kids go into a photo room. The two little boys are in dark gray suits with red bowties and shiny black shoes. Adorable. The baby girl, being held by her mother, has on a red headband with a bow and a red poufy dress with wings on the back. When she turns a little, I see what the baby has in one of her hands—a foam, one-piece bow and arrow. A baby Cupid.

Ugh. Cupid is everywhere.

The door to the room opens, and I finally see him.

"Hey!" Hayden says, and for a split second of sheer panic I think he's talking to me, but I quickly realize he is talking to the kids, so I relax. He looks amazing in his jeans, black loafers and black button-down shirt with a loose-fitting white tie. He squats down to the boys' level, his smile contagious. "You two ready to rock?"

The boys nod and nibble on their fingers.

"Cool! So you guys can be my assistants, all right?"

"Yes!"

"Awesome. I'll especially need help with your sister, okay?"

They're all smiles now. I can't help but smile, too.

He high-fives each one, and then after they decide which background and props to use, pats the table, which is covered with a blanket. "Hop up on here, guys."

Hayden guides them each up and poses them. Then he shuts the door, only it doesn't close all the way, so I walk up closer and peek inside while the bustle of the waiting area is busier than ever. The mom places the baby between the two boys, and Hayden claps his hands while standing behind the camera. The baby smiles, and so do the boys, so he snaps a few photos.

"Excellent!" he praises.

Next, he poses them differently, this time with the baby holding her bow and arrow. Hayden goes back behind the camera and shakes a maraca. All three of them giggle, and he snaps some more. I can see all the photos on a TV-type monitor, set up on a stand in the room.

Things go super well until after about ten minutes. That's when the baby decides she's finished. She wants to get down, and when one of her brothers takes the bow and arrow, she begins to cry. Hayden scrambles in a bin and takes out a teddy bear. Shakes it in front of her. Nothing. Next, he tries a funny elephant puppet and speaks to her in a cutesy voice. "Smile! Smile at the camera!" but this only seems to make her cry more, and her hand flies upward and smacks one of the boys in the eye, which makes him cry. While the mom is trying to calm them down, and while Hayden is shaking a tambourine and tap dancing to get their attention, the other brother hops off the box and reaches for the monitor. He pushes a button and—*poof*—the monitor goes blank.

"Oh, no," Hayden says. While he fumbles with the computer, the boys are taking all the props out of the bins and the baby begins to scream. The frazzled mom lifts her and takes her out of the room, shushing and rocking her as she brushes past me.

As much as I feel sorry for the mom, and also for Hayden, I slink back behind the partially opened door and peek with one eye through the small opening as Hayden finally gets the monitor back on, and thankfully, the pictures he took pop up, too. He turns to the boys. "Let's do that again!" he says, and he poses them one last time; I guess to try and save the session. They sit still long enough for him to make them laugh, and he quickly snaps a few more pics that I can see on the monitor. They really are cute.

When the pictures are finished, the mom tells Hayden how happy she is with the photos. I have to admit, I'm impressed myself. When she leaves to speak to a sales associate to order her photos, Hayden tidies up the room, and a few moments later, he steps out. He looks as frazzled as the mom did a few minutes ago, his tie now halfway undone, and it looks like a button is missing from his shirt. He takes a deep breath and runs his hands through his hair.

And he looks hot.

I clear my throat, and he looks my way. It takes a second, and then he smiles. Really big. "Claire."

I swallow hard and then smile, too. "Hey."

He comes over. "Have you been here long?"

"Long enough."

"You saw that?"

I nod.

"Yikes."

"No," I say. "You totally handled that well. I would have lost my cool in about five-point-two seconds."

When Hayden laughs, his eyes sparkle.

Stop it! I tell myself, sensing Cupid and his bow hovering nearby.

"I just have to clock out," Hayden says. "Be right there."

As I wait, I check my hair in my phone camera. It takes forever for him to come out of the back room.

"Ready?" he finally says when he comes out. He guides me past more over-energetic kids waiting to abuse the next photographer.

"You must be glad you're not dealing with the rest of them in there," I say as we exit into the mall.

Hayden shrugs. "It's not so bad. Once you get used to it."

We walk slowly. Just like Evan, I'm not sure what to do with my hands. Not that I'd want to hold his hand or anything. Speaking of, I wonder where Evan and Leah are. I pull out my cell and send him a quick text.

"I'm sorry," I tell Hayden. "I just have to see where my brother is. He's here with a girl and I'm supposed to be chaperoning."

"What a good big sister," he says, and then he quickly adds, "He is your *younger* brother, right?"

I laugh. "Yeah, he's thirteen."

"Cute. The dude's got a girlfriend already?"

"Believe that?"

I send my text, just: **You okay?** and I'm relieved when he answers fast: **Yup {{:-)**

The smiley-face with wagging eyebrows freaks me out a little —the thought of my baby brother kissing a girl is just...ew.

"So this is your dinner break?" I ask.

"Yeah, but I'm not really hungry. I mean, unless you are. I can always eat. I'll do whatever you want."

I'm actually way too nervous to eat. "I could go for a latte," I say.

"Me too." He smiles again. That's something I could definitely get used to. "Sounds great."

We arrive at Starbucks. I realize how much better it is to be here with him now, without any kind of underwear hanging off my leg. He points to the store across the way. "Hey, you want to make a stuffed animal?"

"Huh?" I follow his finger to see that place where you stuff your own animal and give it a heart and a name and you also get an adoption certificate.

"Build-A-Bear? Really?" I say. Hayden's smile is so corny it's funny. "I've always wanted to do that anyway," I say. "But isn't it expensive?"

Hayden takes out his wallet and fishes out a slip of paper. "Coupon. Half off."

Why is he carrying a coupon for Build-A-Bear? Also, I'm even more confused about him than before. How can he be so sweet... I mean, taking me to Build-A-Bear? All while talking to this other chick and being deceitful? I don't get it.

He must have picked up on my confusion because he says, "It's a mall employee perk. I usually take my sister here."

"How old is your sister?"

"Jenna's eight." Before I can ask if he has any more siblings, he says, "I've got two younger sisters, actually. Chloe's thirteen, too."

"Cool," I say.

"They don't keep all their stuffed animals, though. They usually donate them to a children's hospital. We got the idea when Chloe was admitted with a bad virus. She's better now, but seeing some of those sick kids gave me that idea."

"Wow, Hayden. That's so thoughtful."

"It's the least I could do, or anyone. Right?"

I nod and feel warm all over. That's the nicest thing I've ever heard anyone do.

We stroll through the front area of Build-A-Bear, where you can pick what type of animal you'd like. I look over the dogs, cats, bears, even a frog. While I'm looking at the smaller ones, Hayden picks up a giant monkey skin. I raise one eyebrow, and he shrugs.

"What? I love monkeys!" he says.

"Me too, but isn't that one kind of big?"

"You can't have a big enough monkey."

I laugh at that and then cover my mouth with my hand. Now my face is on fire.

But Hayden laughs, too, so I relax. He puts the giant monkey skin down and picks up a much smaller one. "How's this? Better?"

"Yes. Perfect."

Together we bring it to the person who fills it, and Hayden asks for two hearts to be inserted. I blush at how adorable that is, but I'm also perturbed at the way the girl smiles at Hayden. I look to see if he's smiling back at her. He is.

Why do I care? I straighten my shoulders.

Once the monkey is filled, both hearts in place, we pick out an outfit. I feel silly being a teenager among all the kids here, but this is fun.

"How about these?" Hayden lifts overalls. Of course. A monkey in overalls. I nod and reach for a pair of Keds-style sneakers, holding them up.

"Awesome," he says. At the cash register, Hayden pays, after a hefty discount. "Now he needs a name," he says. "What do you think about Chuck?"

"Nah. That reminds me of that old movie. The one with the creepy doll."

"Good point."

"I have one. Promise not to laugh?"

He looks at me. "Never. What is it?"

"Mooks."

"Mooks?" Hayden bites his lip.

"You said you wouldn't laugh!"

He stifles it, sort of, and pretends to lock his lips and toss the key away.

"Stop laughing," I chide. "I used to have a stuffed bunny that my favorite uncle gave me," I say. "And I wanted to name it after him, but I couldn't pronounce his name. So it came out as Mooks and it stuck."

"Mm mm mm?" Hayden mumbles.

"Huh?"

He points to his locked lips.

I laugh. "Oh. You can unlock."

He pretends to pick up the key and unlocks his lips. "What's his name?"

"Lucas."

Hayden is clearly having a rough time keeping a straight face.

I teasingly tap his extremely muscular arm. "Stop!"

He lets out a full laugh now.

"It's not funny!" I say, but now I'm laughing along with him.

Finally, he straightens up, growing slightly more serious. "Wow, you really had a speech impediment, huh?"

"I was only two!"

He gives me a one-armed hug, and I tense up, feeling his arm wrapped around my shoulders. "I'm only joking," he says. "I think Mooks is a cool name."

He hands everything to me, the monkey in a house-shaped box, and we exit the store, the proud new parents of Mooks the Monkey.

"That was fun," I say, still tingly from his half-hug. "Thanks."

"I'll make monkey business with you any time," he says and then quickly glances at me. "Sorry." He winces. "Too much monkey humor?"

"A little." My face must be redder than Evan's must've been before when he tried to hold Leah's hand. Speaking of Evan, I check my cell for texts. He sent one: **Doing fine. At Spencer's.**

"My brother again," I say to Hayden and then I send Evan a quick reply: **Ok.**

"I'm glad you like the monkey."

"I do." I hold up the box.

"That big one would've been awesome," Hayden says. "I mean, if someone wanted to show you how much they cared via a stuffed animal, that one would make the best impact."

"True. If you're into huge stuffed animals."

Hayden takes my hand in his. I can't help but stiffen again, but I let him. "Yeah," he says nonchalantly. "That'd be true monkey love." He laughs at this as he rubs my hand with his thumb. I'm feeling suddenly lightheaded. This was supposed to only be coffee. Maybe a slice of pizza. Suddenly we're holding hands and we're parents of a monkey.

He must sense my tension, because he tightens his grip a little. "You okay?"

I lead us toward a storefront, out of the way of passersby. I pull my hand from his. "I—I can't accept this," I say, handing him the box.

Hayden looks perplexed, but amused. "You can't accept my monkey?"

"No."

"Why not?"

"It's just... I can't handle what it implies."

"Huh?" Hayden's eyebrows come together. "I think it implies rompy-fun-ness. Doesn't it?"

"I...it's...I just can't take it. Sorry. This was probably a mistake, coming here, doing this."

"Claire, wait." There's a spark in his face, a look of growing concern. "I'm sorry...did I miss something? What's this all about?"

I take a deep breath and blurt it all out, but keep my eyes focused on my sneakers. "Like I said, I'm just out of a relationship and I'm just not ready for a commitment like this, not yet, and I—"

"Claire?"

I look up. His face is soft. Kind. "I know. And it's only a stuffed monkey."

He stares at me for a few seconds. I don't know what to say or do. I'm embarrassed all over again.

"Oh my gosh," I say. "I'm sorry. That was so dumb."

He holds up a hand. "It's cool. No worries. I mean that. But Mooks here wants to know if you're still going to take him home. Or he'll be a homeless, orphaned monkey."

I smile. "Yeah. I'll take him home."

"Good." He leans down and yells into the box. "You hear that, Mooks? Claire's taking you home!"

We begin to walk again, and when we reach The Photo Shoot, we stop at the entrance. I look up at him. "I'm just scared," I say.

"I know. I totally get it."

"Are you scared of anything?" I ask.

He thinks a moment. "Heights."

"Me too."

"What else?"

"Public speaking," I tell him about the speech I was supposed to give in sixth grade and how I flubbed it and froze up in front of the whole school. "So I ran off the stage. Everyone was laughing. And the irony was that the assembly was about facing your fears and believing in yourself."

"That *is* ironic," Hayden says. After a pause, he says, "If it helps, I'm also terrified of clowns."

"Who *isn't* scared of those?"

He shrugs. "Other clowns?"

From inside, Hayden's manager waves him in. It looks to me like there are more unruly kids and frazzled parents than before.

"It was fun hanging out with you, Claire," he says. He lifts my hand and kisses it. Every cell in my body screams. "I hope to see you again sometime very soon…But no pressure!" he adds fast with a big smile.

This makes me giggle. "No pressure," I say back.

My feet feel glued to the floor as I watch him leave. I know I have to move eventually, but all I can do is stand here and think that I can't do this. Relationships suck. They always end in tragedy. Just ask Romeo and Juliet.

So why am I allowing myself to fall for him? I'm only going to get hurt.

I wish I had an answer to that.

CHAPTER THIRTEEN

For the rest of the week, I do everything I can to keep myself from reliving my monkey freak-out session with Hayden. Why did I act like such a weirdo? The guy was just being nice, and I nearly ruined it by acting like a psycho.

I can't stop thinking about April though. I don't even know her, but she keeps invading my headspace. Is he with her right now? If he is, he's a good actor. He was so sweet to me the other night. So much so that dealing with Liv and listening to her talk about the dance, or Andy, or even watching Josh and Briana making out by Josh's locker didn't bother me much.

But Saturday is another story. This is the day he asked April to go to the party at his friend's house. I wonder what he'll do when she never shows up. Will he be upset? Angry? Disappointed? I wish I could go—in disguise, of course. Then I could get a glimpse of what's going on.

Who am I lately?

I'm a person who is looking out for herself, that's who.

Saturday night, Mom, Dad, and Evan are eating popcorn with sprinkled cheese and watching movies.

"Come watch with us, Claire Bear," Dad offers. I'm about to

say no thanks, but they all look so cozy on the sofa with pillows and blankets everywhere. It'll be a good distraction, I tell myself, because Liv's babysitting tonight and couldn't sleep over, and Hayden's waiting for April to show up. I sigh and plop between Mom and Dad, glad my cell phones are up in my room.

After three bowls of popcorn and three movies, I'm super tired, so I say goodnight to my family and head upstairs to bed. When I get there, the first thing I notice is that I have a bunch of messages from Hayden—to April.

My heart sinks into my stomach. I don't want to, but I open them and read.

Hey. You coming?

Just wondering if you're on your way.

Mark says to say hi. ;)

April? You there?

I guess you got busy? Text me tomorrow.

MONDAY, I decide to skip eating my PB&B sandwich in the girls' room and, instead, sit with Liv at lunch. I need to stop rehashing those text messages Hayden wrote to April.

When I sit at our table, Liv stares at me, her French fry halfway to her mouth. "What's wrong?"

"Nothing. Why?"

"I can tell it's something. Spill it."

God, she's good.

"Nothing, I'm just, I don't know...tired." I really am. I hardly slept last night. Or the night before. I'd love to tell her about Hayden now that I'm sure she had nothing to do with my meeting him. But I know that if I did, she'd never leave me alone about him. And right now, I'm not even sure what to do, and I can't think if she's firing off of a billion questions. Besides, she'd make an excuse for his actions and probably confuse me more.

Liv bites her fry and is still eyeballing me. I look at my sandwich. Take small pieces off and chew them. I feel her eyes boring into me, but I can't talk about Hayden now. I hope she looks away soon.

She doesn't. She's staring at me intently, squinty eyes and all. "Hmm," she says, chewing. She swallows. "I don't believe you, but when you're ready to talk, here I am. Oh, and we need to get to the mall." She grabs another fry, pops it into her mouth.

"The mall? Why? Why do we need to go to the mall?"

"Why are you so paranoid?"

"What? I'm not, I'm—"

"I need a dress for the dance. It's Saturday, remember?"

"Oh, sure, I remember."

I'm so glad when Kevin Walsh and Miles Greenberg come over and sit on each side of her, both vying for her attention and distracting her from me. I'm never envious of her in a bad way. I just wish I could be as confident and comfortable around guys as she is.

That's it. That's my new-*new* wish.

Just then, I notice Andy standing beside me.

"Hey, Claire," he says. "Hi, Liv."

"Hey," Liv says from across the table.

Andy takes a seat beside me. "Hey, so, Claire," he says in a low voice. "Can I talk to you?"

"Isn't that what you're already doing?" I say.

"Yeah, yeah. Sorry." He looks down at his hands.

"Oh, wow. Sorry. I have to remind myself that people don't always get my sarcasm."

"It's okay," he says with a nervous laugh. "I meant, can we talk, you know, alone?"

I can feel Liv staring our way. "Maybe over there?" Andy points with his chin to the corner of the cafeteria, to an empty table.

"Sure." We get up and cross the room, and I can still feel Liv watching. She must be dying.

"So, I, um…" Andy begins, once we sit down. He takes a breath, slowly lets it out, and then says, "Well, I'm, uh, thinking that, uh…"

"Look, Andy," I say, feeling Liv's eyeballs boring into me. "I'm not ready to date anyone right now, especially after the break-up I just went through." I wave my hand, trying to make less of it than it really is. "And even though I met this new guy, it was a totally random thing, and I know I met up with him, but it wasn't really a date-date—it was more of a mall-friendly-meet-up type of thing. I mean, we made a stuffed animal, but I'm not exactly sure if I'll ever see him again now, and if I *were* to meet him again, I'd—"

"Claire?" Andy's staring as if he has no clue as to why I've just wigged out.

I smile sheepishly. "Sorry." I laugh, but it comes out sounding more maniacal than I intended. I snap my mouth shut.

"It's okay," he says, and now *he* looks at *me* sympathetically. Ugh, I have a feeling this is going to end badly. "I was just wondering if…this is so hard…if you could maybe talk to Liv?"

"Liv?"

"I mean, talk to her for me? So I can ask her out?"

Oh, that. I open and close my mouth, false starts and stops, trying to think of what to say to that, all while my cheeks burn with embarrassment. I want to melt right off this chair and into the tiled floor.

Andy's eyes go big, and he grips both of my hands in his. "Oh, I'm sorry. Did you think I was asking you out? I didn't mean to get your hopes up."

"What?" I snap to and slip my hands away from his. "No, you didn't get my hopes up! Of course not! I *totally* knew what you were about to ask me. About Liv. And yes, of course I'll talk to her about you. Sheesh." I still want to melt into the floor.

Andy relaxes and leans back in his chair. "Oh. Good. I thought you thought that I was—"

I hold up my hand to stop him. "Yeah, I heard you the first time. It's all good."

"Phew." Andy wipes his brow. I don't think I ever saw anyone do that before unless they're a mime. I want to laugh but I don't want to hurt his feelings. Now I don't know where to look. Or where to put my hands. I decide to sit on them.

"I'm glad we got that cleared up," he says.

Yeah, you wouldn't want to ask me out by mistake, I want to say. But I refrain.

After a few more awkward, trying-to-think-of-things-to-talk-about moments, the bell rings.

PHEW! I mentally wipe my brow.

"Thanks, Claire," he says, patting my shoulder. "I owe you one."

"Yeah, yeah, no problem," I say as he stands up. "See you around."

"Seriously," he says. "I've been crushing on her forever. I even sent her an anonymous Cupid-gram."

"That was you?"

"Well, it wasn't me. It was a Cupid gram-er. Did you see it? You're in her bio class, right?"

"Yeah. But no, I didn't see it. I actually walked past the guy as he went in."

"I'm not sure I want to tell her it was from me. You won't tell her, will you?"

"Not if you don't want me to. And I think that was sweet of you." I stand now too and then push my chair back under the table.

"Thanks, Claire. If you ever need a favor, I'm here."

"Good to know. See ya." I wiggle my fingers in a small wave and head back toward Liv. From what I can tell, Andy seems like he might be a good guy. If there are even any good ones left in the world besides my dad. And maybe Evan.

Maybe.

CHAPTER FOURTEEN

"HE WANTS to go out with you," I tell Liv between lunch and study hall. This is my part in the so-called favor I'm doing for Andy. We stop at her locker.

"Really?" Liv says while I watch her turn the combination dial. And is that a look of relief on her face? "I thought he was asking you out."

"I did too...for a split second. Talk about embarrassing."

She gets what she needs and closes the locker door.

"Are you okay now?" she asks.

"Who, me? Sure. I'm fine. I was upset about my mom's salon. It's been slow, and she's been worried, so I'm worried, too." It's mostly true; it's just not what I was thinking about today at lunch.

Liv pouts. "Maybe we can drum up some business for her. Everyone loves the way she does my color. I'll remind everyone again of when she's working. Maybe your mom can give a slight discount to them. Give them more of a reason to come in."

How great is she? And how sucky am I as a friend? I won't even tell her about my new...crush or whatever Hayden is to me. My new secret? That works.

"Thanks, Liv."

We head down the hall.

"So?" I say at the stairs, before we part ways. "Do you want to go out with him?"

"I don't know, I'll think about it."

Liv's got such a poker face and usually never shows her hand until the last minute, but right now, there's a sparkle in her eyes and I recall a certain smile she gave when they said hi the other day. It was different than the smiles she gives any other guy.

"We have to make guys sweat it out, Claire," she says as if she can read my mind. "So I guess I should keep him guessing. Tell him I'll think about it. See you in bio. Love you." She kisses my cheek and off she trots up the steps.

LATER IN ENGLISH CLASS, Ms. Levine tells us we're watching a movie. Mentally, I pump my fist in the air.

She adds that it's a shortened version of *A Midsummer Night's Dream*, which prompts groans all around, but I'm okay with that since I'm trying hard to pass this class. She rolls in an ancient TV on a stand with a VCR player beneath it and pops in the tape. It's jumpy at first, but it finally starts playing properly, and she flicks off the lights.

The play is in black and white, and I can hardly concentrate, which you really have to do when trying to follow Shakespeare, what with deciphering between the *thees* and the *thous*. Not to mention trying to decipher some of his lines: *Love looks not with the eyes, but with the mind, and therefore is winged Cupid painted blind.*

I totally get that one, though. Cupid's totally blind. "That's why he makes so many mistakes," I say under my breath.

I'm half listening while the other half of my brain is thinking about how embarrassed I felt with Andy before, and then about my non-date with Hayden and the freaky monkey outburst thing, and then I realize I went a whole day without thinking about Josh, unless you count now, but that's not the same thing.

Then, about three-quarters of the way through the play, something catches my attention. It's how Helena chases Demetrius (yes, she actually chases him!), and I realize I'm a lot like her. Not that I ever chased after Josh, but there have been a few times when I wanted to rush down the hall and tackle him. Make him see what he's been missing.

But now I'm beginning to realize I can't force him to love me (unless he's under a Shakespearean spell). And maybe he wasn't always happy with me. I guess he deserves to be happy, too. But maybe in the future, he should go about finding happiness in a better way, as in not cheating with his girlfriend's best friend. So not cool.

I'm in such deep thought that I don't realize the movie has stopped until Ms. Levine turns on the lights and everyone groans and squints at the sudden greenish spark of light flooding the room.

"Books under your desks, please," she announces, which means a flash quiz. Great. I was off in dreamland during half the movie, so I hope it's not too in-depth. There's more grunting as papers are handed back, row by row, and books are slipped under chairs. When I get the sheet and look it over, I see it's got five questions that are to be answered in our own words. I zip through the test, but pause at the last question.

1. *What part of her appearance does Hermia accuse Helena of exploiting to win over Lysander? Explain in your words why you think Hermia was upset.*

The answer is easy-peasy. It's her height. But this sends me on a whole new wave of thoughts. Hermia was beautiful and both guys loved and wanted her. Neither wanted Helena, but when the chips were down and after the spells were cast, Hermia accused

Helena of using her taller height to woo the guys. As if Helena could help that. Seriously, what a brat Hermia was. I know she was freaking out over her boyfriend's sudden change of heart, but did she want beauty, brains, love, *and* height, too? Some girls want everything.

The bell rings before I can fully write my answer, and Ms. Levine demands that we stop and pass our papers up toward the front of the room. Not finishing will give me twenty-percent less of a score than if I'd written the stupid answer down.

Geez. Love even interferes with my schoolwork.

CHAPTER FIFTEEN

DAD'S MAKING homemade pizza Monday night. He's using his own sauce, which he makes and freezes ahead of time in plastic bags. He should have been a chef instead of a realtor. I don't ever tell him that anymore, though, because I discovered, after hearing Mom talking to my grandma, that he sacrificed opening his own restaurant so that Mom could open her hair salon. Over the last few years, business has gone down for her, but my dad never, ever complains. He just tries to sell more houses.

He turns when I come into the kitchen. He's humming some Italian melody, The Tarantella, I think it's called, and I smile but only a little because I'm still disappointed about the test.

"Claire Bear," he says, turning to me fully. He drops the pizza dough and, humming again, takes me on a spin, linking arms. He spins me and then takes me in the other direction, linking my left arm.

"Daaaad," I whine, but secretly, I love it.

He takes both of my hands and spins me around. Then, at the last part of the song, he yells "Hey!" and leans me backward into a dramatic dip.

I look up at his flour-covered face and laugh. "Are we done?" I ask.

"*Si, signorina.*" He helps me to stand, and I brush the flour off my jeans.

"Sorry 'bout that," he says. "Got caught up in the moment."

He offers me a square of fresh mozzarella. "Forgive me?"

I nearly swallow the cheese whole, it's so good. "Sure. And the mozzarella helps. Cheese makes everything better," I say.

Dad pouts and tilts his head a little. "You needed cheese? Are you okay?"

"Yeah, I think I got an 80 on a quiz today."

"That's not so bad."

"It is when you knew it could be a 95 or 100."

"At least you're trying," he says as I help bring plates and utensils into the dining room. "Oh, take out an extra setting for Leah."

"She's coming for dinner?" I ask. "Are you kidding? Evan's *thirteen*. Since when? I had to wait 'til...I'm still not allowed to have a boyfriend over!" Okay, I exaggerated that last part. But I was only allowed this past year to have Josh over. And I was almost sixteen.

Later we're all around the table. Small talk ensues, broken by lots of comments over how good the food is.

"Oh, Mom," I say. "There's a school dance on Saturday."

"On Valentine's Day?"

I nod.

"How sweet," she coos. "You're going? And why didn't you tell me sooner?"

"I've been trying to figure a way to bail, but I told Liv that I would go back in September. I can't do that to her. So I won't be able to work that day. Okay?"

"Sure," she says, and I can tell she's a little relieved. I'll be one less person to pay that day, even though I haven't worked in weeks now.

The conversation switches to Dad's job as I grab another slice of pizza and then a little more salad. That's when I notice Evan reach for Leah's hand. They link fingers and then drop their hands under the table. I smirk to myself; this is definitely ammo for teasing him later. They're sharing looks, sweet little smiles, and whispering to while Mom and Dad talk to each other, too.

I'm sitting here at the table, the lone-man-out, and I don't know what to do with myself. Drown myself in the iced tea? Gorge myself on more pizza? I stab a forkful of lettuce and shove it into my mouth. I chew, but hardly taste my food as I look around the room at all of this...love.

That's when one of my phones buzzes from inside my pocket. I slip them out and unlock the screen of my newer one without my parents seeing. My heart summersaults when I see Hayden's name. I open the text. **Thinking of u. Wanna hang out tomorrow? Just friends. :)**

He's referencing my monkey freak-out from the other night. How dare he be cute when he's talking to some other girl? Who never answered, by the way. And he's not texted her since either. Maybe he's given up on her and I'm second best.

That just makes me angry. I type back: **Can't, sorry.** As mad as I am right now, my shoulders still deflate at that.

:(Ok. Another day?

Sure.

Yeah. Right. The fifth of Neverary.

I stab a baby tomato. Juice and seeds squirt out. It's a metaphor for my heart. Stabbed. Crushed. Damaged. Why do guys cheat?

Disgusted, I imagine Cupid sitting here with me. If I could speak to him, I'd say, "How dare you make me feel hopeful only to stomp on my heart again?" Tears build in my eyes. I get up so fast my chair nearly topples. I catch it just in time, but now everyone is silent and looking up at me.

"You okay?" Mom asks a few seconds later.

"Yeah. Sorry. Carry on." I bring my dishes to the kitchen and begin to wash them, scrubbing hard as conversations resume in the dining room. I imagine Cupid sitting on the edge of the sink now, his chubby legs dangling just above the sudsy water. He waves his stupid bow at me.

"Go away!" I say. I laugh as I imagine him losing his balance and falling into the water.

"Claire?" Mom calls from the dining room. "Did you say something?"

Did I just say that out loud? I'm losing it.

"No!" I call over my shoulder. Under my breath, I add, "Just trying to terminate Cupid."

And then I turn on the garbage disposal.

CHAPTER SIXTEEN

ON MONDAY I discover I was right about my test. I only got an 80. But I got an extra two points because Ms. Levine liked my thoughtful answers for questions 1 through 4, so at least it's not a 78. Go, me.

I've been contemplating calling Hayden back. Since Friday, he's texted five times. Not in a stalky kind of way (i.e.: creeping from behind bra displays at Victoria's Secret) but in a friendly, not-trying-too-hard kind of way. Sort of like: **Hey, how are you?** and **Did you catch the last American Horror Story episode? Sick!** I feel badly that I haven't answered with anything more than one-word answers or just a smiley face. I know he has no clue that I'm upset even though I shouldn't be. I should be glad this is happening. I don't want a boyfriend and to have my heart broken into a million pieces again. Maybe this will keep that from happening before I get in too deep with him.

But the truth is, I'm already in too deep.

During lunch, I skip the cafeteria and slip into the upstairs girls' room, where I get a message. It's Hayden texting April. My heart sinks to the floor. I have to answer.

Hey there.

Hey, I write, thinking of what I could say next. Fighting tears, I first come up with *Buzz off, you have a sort-of girlfriend who seems to like you, and you're a creep for wanting to mess with me!* But I can't write that. April and I don't even know each other. So I just write: **Sorry I didn't get back 2 u sooner...had to study for a trig test. Oh, and sorry about Saturday. Couldn't make the party.**

While I wait for his reply, I think of something profound to say other than lying about trig. I mean, I don't even *take* trigonometry.

That's okay, he answers. **Hope you aced the test. ;)**

I did, I say back.

We missed you at the party.

Who's we?

If I ask, would he be like: **???** because April should know who he means? I send a shoulder-shrugging emoji and wait for another response, which comes a moment later.

I'd love to get together and talk again. I need advice.

Again? And advice for what? I need to know. So *I* send: **???**

We'll talk in person. Let me know when you're around.

I'm not sure how to answer that, and my imagination is making up all kinds of scenarios, so before it makes me completely insane, I shut off my phone and shove it into my purse. My eyes fill with tears despite my trying to hold them back, and I toss my sandwich in the trash. It takes a few minutes to collect myself, and then I spend the rest of the period fixing my smeary mascara with a wet tissue.

I'm tempted to call Mom and ask her to come and get me but she always knows when I'm upset, just like Liv does. She'll ask too many questions.

After ninth period, Liv meets me at my locker. "Where were you during lunch? Why is your phone turned off? Is it dead? And why were you so late for Algebra?"

See what I mean? Questions.

"Cramps," I say. "I hung at the nurse's for a while. And my phone was off."

"Oh. You're still going to the decorations committee meeting today, right?" It's like this day keeps getting better and better. "We're going over the budget and the plan for what we need to buy for the dance," she adds as I rummage through my locker and take out my jacket. "We need the help with all the paper hearts we're cutting out so we can dangle them from the ceiling."

"Can we have a contest to see who can shoot the most down with Cupid arrows?" I say and close the locker door.

Liv stares at me for a moment. "What? Why would we do that?"

"Sorry. Never mind," I say. "Of course I'll come. Wouldn't miss it."

"Thanks, Claire. Actually, Cupid arrows are an awesome idea. We can make those, too."

I resist the urge to slap myself on the forehead while we walk toward the gym and Liv rattles on and on about the dance, lists, and budgets. When we get there, I text Mom to tell her I'm taking the late bus home today, and when I look back up, I see Andy. He waves us over to a table where he's sitting with a few other people. Small groups sit at tables spread around the gym, doing various jobs like cutting and coloring and gluing, with upperclassmen handing out scissors and poster boards.

Andy says "hey" to me when we approach his table, but he's looking at Liv. I take a seat as a senior named Madison shows me and Liv how to cut out red poster board hearts. I roll my eyes. It's not like we're in kindergarten.

"This dance is going to be awesome," Liv says once we get started.

For the next few minutes, I notice Liv sneaking glances at Andy. When she's distracted by someone asking her a question, Andy leans over to me. "Did you ask her?" he whispers.

Just then Josh and Briana enter the gym. They're standing by the door. Josh squeezes her hand. Briana smiles and rests her head on his shoulder.

I crush the heart I was working on with both hands. When I realize Andy's looking at me as if he just witnessed me murder Cupid himself, I take a deep breath and say, "That one came out really bad. And I did speak to her."

"Really?"

"Yes, and I think she likes you, too. She just won't admit it."

Andy's face lights up. That's when I get an idea. I can build on Liv's idea, actually, and turn things around a little. Liv deserves to be happy, too. I know she can have her pick of almost any guy, but now that I think about it, she doesn't ever pick any of them. Is that because she's scared? If so, of what? What could be holding her back? Suddenly, I'm thinking back over all the years I've known her, and that's when I realize she's never had a steady boyfriend. She's always liked this boy or that boy, but never had an actual relationship.

Why hadn't I noticed this before? Maybe it's because I've been too wrapped up in myself all this time. Well, not anymore. She's always been there for me, always helped me out. Now I want to help her, and this plan will help me stop thinking about April and Hayden.

"You're going to take her to the dance, Andy," I say.

His eyebrows go up. "You think—?"

"Yes!"

"I don't understand. How do you know she wants to go with me?"

"Trust me, I know. She doesn't let on about her feelings. But I think it's time for me to play Cupid. If I can't beat him, I'll join him."

Andy looks confused at first, so I fill him in on the rest of my idea, which is to make her jealous when she thinks he's into me. Hopefully, it'll make her admit she has feelings for him. Plus, as a bonus, it'll make Josh think I'm into someone else. And that can't hurt.

"Okay, if you think it'll work. You are her best friend."

"It totally will. And it'll help me, too, to give Josh and Briana a little dig. See those two over there? Look, but don't look."

Andy inconspicuously glances their way, and I brief him. "Josh is the ex I started to tell you about the other day, who, while I was still with him, got together with Briana—who was my *best friend at the time*."

Andy winces. "Ouch."

"Yeah. Ouch. So I want to make him see that I've moved on. And that I'm happy. Maybe rub it in a little. That's all, no harm done. Just a little lie. And that part about Josh was Liv's idea, by the way, so she shouldn't be mad."

As I hatch my plan and discuss it with Andy I realize I could've brought Hayden to the dance and not only would it make Josh jealous, I might have actually been happy. But not now.

Andy pauses while cutting out a big red heart. "Don't get mad at what I'm about to say."

Uh-oh. He's bailing, I bet.

"I'll help you out, but I don't think you have to do all of this, Claire. You're super pretty and smart and any guy would be lucky to be with you."

I look up at him. Really? I'm shocked. Is that who I am? Am I like Helena? Am I that insecure about my own worth?

I really do need to work on my confidence.

"Thanks," I say, feeling my face flush. "I guess I want to make him feel the way he made me feel."

"I get that," he says, nodding. "But is he worth it?"

We both look over at him and Briana, who are laughing and holding hands. Maybe it's not worth it. Maybe I should just move on. But revenge is sweet sometimes. And so is playing Cupid.

"This is more for Liv's benefit," I say. "And yours." Really, just like in *Midsummer Night's Dream*, there are so many relationship mix-ups around me. It worked in the play, so why can't it work in real life? It's worth a try. And it's all in the name of love. *You hear that, Cupid?*

Andy smiles. "Okay, then."

I grab a Cupid cutout lying on the table and hold it up. "Let Project Jealousy commence."

He holds one up, too. "Project Jealousy!" he whisper-yells.

"Good. Now, pretend you're into me," I say.

Andy is facing Liv, and I can tell he's half watching her as he glances at me. And from my vantage point, I see Josh and Briana, too. I pour on the confidence. Flip my hair. Sit up straight, shoulders back. Laugh a lot. Just like them.

I get a sudden burst of inspiration, grab Andy's shirt collar, and pull him toward me. "Kiss me!" I say.

"What?"

"Josh is looking. Kiss me!"

Andy finally gets it. He comes in for the kill, a little too fast, and kisses me hard on the mouth, nearly knocking me off my seat.

As we kiss, (closed-mouthed—I won't go further just for jealousy) I open my eyes and see Josh quickly look down and then back up with only his eyes peering through his hair. Then he looks back down again.

Andy pulls away and glances behind me, I assume, toward Liv. He seems worried.

"Don't stop," I tell him. "Just remember, if she looks upset, it's working."

I'll explain to Liv later that I only kissed Andy because of what she suggested to me, and how I got carried away with the kiss, and that it meant nothing to me. But for now, I can't waste any time. I'm aware that we're being watched like we're playing tennis.

For once, the ball's in my court. It feels good to see Josh seem uncomfortable. I turn to give Liv the thumbs-up, but she's sitting there with her mouth slightly open, her eyes open wider than usual. Shoot. Did I take things too far?

"Did it work with Josh, too?" Andy asks me, breaking my thoughts. I turn and see that, across the room, Josh is staring at me.

"Yup."

Briana also turns in my direction and then back to Josh, where she probably makes the connection. Point one: me.

Briana says something to him. He answers. In a few seconds, they look like they're arguing. I can tell by the way arms begin to flail and Briana points a finger at him. Josh stands and storms out of the gym. Briana seems pissed, and then she gets up and runs after him.

Smiling, I lean back in my chair. I've done what I've set out to do. Point, match. Or is it: two, love? Either way, I'm winning.

CHAPTER SEVENTEEN

LIV and I are waiting for the late buses outside the school after the decoration committee meeting ends. I've just finished explaining how awesome it was to make Josh jealous. "It worked. You were so right," I tell her, and then I explain how awesome her advice was. I feel really good, too, like I'm even getting back at Hayden.

So why do I also feel like total crap at the same time?

"Are you okay, Liv?"

"I'm fine."

"You don't seem fine."

She looks me in the eye. Hers are glassy. "It was my idea for you to make Josh jealous, and I get that. But did it have to be with Andy?"

I can't help but smile. "You like him, don't you?"

She sniffles and shrugs one shoulder.

"You know that was only an act, right, Liv?"

She nods.

I should be happy, proud even, but my guilt overpowers either of those feelings. I don't want to hurt Liv. "I'll never do that again. I promise," I say. "And he really likes you."

Liv lightens up. "He does?"

"A lot."

I give her a hug as the bus pulls up. I'm taking hers home today so her mom can take us to the mall to look for a dress for Liv. Maybe I'll find one, too.

"I *am* glad you're going to the dance," Liv says as we scooch into a seat toward the back. I take the window. "Even though you really don't want to. I love you for coming for me."

"You know I'd do anything for you," I tell her. And I mean it.

"I'm also impressed at how Andy wants to help you. How thoughtful is that of him?"

"Super thoughtful."

"And how cool was it that Josh got so mad?"

"*So* cool."

I stare out the window for a few blocks, reliving how mad Josh seemed. Good for him. Good for Briana, too. But somehow, as good as I feel, I also feel sort of mean. And immature, like the whole thing was a waste of time. Like, it feels good to get revenge, but not that good. Helena in the play never sought revenge. Maybe she should have. I don't know.

I turn my phone on. There aren't any messages from Hayden. I lay my head against the glass. Vibrations from the bus makes it bounce every few seconds but I don't care. I stay that way all the way to Liv's stop.

We make our way off the bus. When we're a few houses away from hers, she says, "What if he fell for you?"

It takes me a second to realize she means Andy. "Me? You're worried he'll like *me*?" I say.

She nods. This reminds me of how Hermia, the beauty who could have anyone, was jealous of her less-than-pretty friend, Helena. Is that what's happening?

"Give me a break, Liv. He's all about you."

"Do you think so?"

"I know so. You're all he talks about."

"I'm sorry," she quickly says as we enter her house. "I'm being paranoid. I don't want you to feel bad. Forget I said that."

I do, but in a small, small way, it feels good to know that she thinks I could steal a guy from her. Even if it isn't true and if I'd never try to do that. In any case, I think it's amazing to play Cupid. For a little bit, anyhow.

Later at the mall, I'm relieved I won't run into Hayden, since it's his day off. So I'm able to relax enough to be myself with Liv, who drags me to four different stores. We look through rack after rack of dresses. But no matter how many dresses I see, and how much I think I'm not going to think about Hayden, my thoughts find their way back to him every time.

I'm not thinking of whether or not these dresses look good on her (they all do). I'm wondering what Hayden's favorite color is, or if he'd think I looked cute in this style or that one.

I eventually find one or two that I like and tell myself that since I'm going to the dance, I may as well try and find a new dress and look cute. Liv picks out a sky-blue baby-doll dress, which she declares makes my eyes pop and doesn't make my arms look chubby. Done and done.

Liv tries on about twenty more dresses. She also doesn't need a new dress, but who wouldn't get something new when their parents insisted? Can't say I blame her. With this last one, she prances out of the fitting room and checks herself in the three-way mirror. She's wearing an adorable knee-length tangerine chiffon-y dress with spaghetti straps.

"So-o-o cute," I say, and I mean it, not just wanting her to get a move on already, as my dad always says.

"You think?" She bites the inside of her cheek, making her face contort as she studies her reflection.

"Adorbs," I say. I check the time on my phone. 6:30 PM. It's time to take action here. "And it's not red, and you look skinny."

She lights up at that. "Sold!"

Thank the dress gods above.

"Listen," I say through the dressing room door as she (finally!) gets dressed. "I could go for a latte. You?"

"Sure," she says, and after we pay for our dresses and start to walk out of the store, Liv stops at the jewelry counter. "Ooh, earrings!" she announces. She starts debating between the dangly rhinestones and the silver hoops. "Oh, wait." She points to a pair of glittery emerald-colored studs.

"Why don't you get your earrings, and I'll meet you at Starbucks when you're done?" I say.

"Okay. Give me half an hour. I want to look at shoes over there, too."

"Perfect." I leave the store with my dress in the plastic bag over my arm. When I get to Starbucks, I can't help but look into The Photo Shoot, even though I know Hayden's not there.

I get my latte. But I don't go back to Liv yet. I walk past The Photo Shoot again, remembering how good he seems to be at his job, like the way he handled those kids the other day.

I'm about to head back to Liv when I see him—Hayden's standing near the back counter of The Photo Shoot, not in uniform, but in jeans, a black t-shirt, and an open denim jacket. He's talking to a girl with long, dark hair. She's in jeans, too, and is carrying her jacket over her arm.

She says something, looks at her phone, and nods. He laughs, throwing his head back, his mouth open. She laughs, too, now, and places her hand on his arm. I scooch over so I can't be seen if he were to look toward the front of the store. There's a little more talking, a little more back-and-forth, and a lot of laughing. A few seconds later, she hugs him. He hugs her back. It lasts forever.

She finally lets him go and turns just enough for me to get a good look at her face. She's gorgeous. I duck into the store I'm in front of, a fancy candle place, and watch them through the display window. Winter Spice and Vanilla candles tickle my nose.

"Um, miss? There's no food or beverages allowed in the store," someone says behind me.

I nod and wave my hand. "Okay, okay," I tell her, but my feet feel like two solid bricks cemented to the floor. They're still talking and laughing. Her hand is on his arm again.

I knew it. No guy is perfect. There's no such thing as a good relationship. Cupid is wrong. Love is stupid.

"Miss?"

I straighten up and storm out of the store, intent on finding Liv and going home. I keep my head down and stare at my coffee cup, willing myself not to cry.

"Claire? Claire!"

I hear his voice. Hayden's spotted me. I stop and look up. He's waving me over. She's looking, too. Smiling. What the heck. I force a smile and will my feet to cooperate.

When I get there, he's all smiles. The girl is even more beautiful up close. I swallow hard and try not to cry, because, seriously. She's got long, silky dark hair, blue-green eyes, smooth skin, and perfect teeth.

Now I want to run a hand over my own hair to smooth it. And what am I even wearing right now? I should've paid more attention to my appearance today. But then, I didn't expect to see Hayden.

"Hey," Hayden says, smiling. "What are you doing here?" He eyes the bag slung over my arm.

"Dresses," I say, lifting it. "My friend and I came for dresses. For the school dance." I lift my coffee next. "And I needed a latte." I take a sip, feeling super awkward.

Hayden looks past me. "Your friend's here?"

"She's still looking for shoes and earrings. I told her I'd meet her in half an hour. So I should get back."

Hayden motions to the gorgeous girl. "This is April. April, Claire."

April. No wonder he's two-timing me.

"Hey," she says to me. She's smiling, and I'm a statue. Completely frozen. Can't speak; in fact, I can barely breathe.

"I love your Vans," she says, pointing to my checkered yellow-and-white sneakers.

Again, I should answer, but I'm still speechless.

Hayden clears his throat. "Are you okay?"

I snap to. I'm not sure what to make of this. He's here on his day off with April—who I've been impersonating. Does he know?

"Claire?" he repeats.

"I-I have to go." My heart is banging its fists on my ribs like a prisoner in a cell.

"Actually, I should go, too," Miss Universe says. "Thanks, Hayden, for everything." With that, she stands on her toes and kisses his cheek.

Kisses. His. Cheek.

She's back down on her heels, and she waggles her fingers at me with a killer smile like some supermodel. "Nice to meet you," she says and walks off, leaving me and Hayden.

I look up at him. *Is he watching her go?*

"She's nice, right?" he says.

I snap to, and the realization of this situation hits me hard. But what can I say? That I know who she is because I've been pretending to be her? I just nod my head.

"My friend likes her," he says.

I want to say, "Right. And is your 'friend' named Hayden?" but instead, I keep nodding.

"I didn't want to tell you in front of her, but she's the one who I was supposed to meet the day you and I met."

Of course I know this. But I say nothing. I bite my lip.

"I came to talk to my manager," he says, "about my schedule, and she happened to come in to see me at the same time. She needed to talk to me about something."

Just so happened, huh? I think about whether there were any messages from him to her today, and there weren't, so maybe this part's true. Unless he's setting me up so I confess. I need to be on my guard.

"And you happened to come to the mall, too," he adds. *Phew!* He doesn't seem to know anything. "I'm glad you did." With that, he leans over and kisses my cheek.

I can't help but wonder, What if he finds out I'm posing as her? Thinking about it now makes my upper lip bead-up in sweat.

"Where are you headed to now?" he asks.

"Liv's waiting for me."

"Mind if I walk with you?"

"No," I say and lead the way.

As we walk, he's talking about work and then about this leather jacket in a store window that catches his eyes, but I'm thinking about how lucky I am that he didn't catch me posing as some other girl and deceiving him. He said that his friend really likes her. I suppose that's possible. But then why did he ask her to that party last Saturday and not me? Was it really for his friend? I'm contemplating all of this while trying to remain cool.

Hayden touches my arm. "Are you all right? You seem so...distant."

As I'm about to answer, Liv calls my name. I turn to see her standing there, a dress slung over her arm. "Hi," she says, looking from me to Hayden and back to me again.

The jig is up. It's time to tell her the truth.

CHAPTER EIGHTEEN

"HAYDEN, THIS IS LIV. LIV, HAYDEN."

If we lived in a cartoon world, a lightbulb would be hovering over Liv's head right now.

Hayden reaches to shake her hand. She takes his hand, but is staring up at him, a look of confusion on her face. She's going to have a bazillion questions for me.

"Hey. It's nice to meet you," he says. When they release each other's hands, Liv finally looks at me. Her face is a giant question mark.

"Hayden and I met here at the mall," I say. "He works at The Photo Shoot, and I just saw him, even though it's his day off, and he walked with me to find you." I don't know why I'm rambling.

"Well, I'd better go. I have a ton of homework. Bye, Liv. Bye, Claire." With that, he kisses my cheek again. I feel myself blush. We watch him go, and Liv is silent. Until she squeals.

"Shh!" I say as people turn to look at us. But she's still squealing. "God, Liv, stop! He'll hear you." I pull her by the arm, away from staring eyes.

"He's *cute*! When did you meet him? Are you two together?

And he just *kissed you*! Why didn't you tell me? I want all the deets!" She's practically hyperventilating.

"Calm down. It was nothing." I point to her and me. "And this is why I didn't tell you. Because I knew you'd do this."

"Sorry. But that was *so not* nothing." She squints at me. "I know you've been keeping things from me."

"What? I have not! Hayden and I are just friends."

"Puh-lease, I saw the way he looked at you."

He did? He looked at me in a certain way?

"Not to mention how red your face got. Now, spill. What are you hiding?"

"I'm not hiding anything! I just met a guy, that's all. No biggie. Come on. Your mom's probably on her way."

We walk, heading to the spot where her mom's supposed to pick us up. There are so many things I should be telling her, sharing with her, but I just don't feel ready to go there yet.

"How did you meet him? Did you go to his store? Why would you go to a photo studio? Did you meet at Starbucks?" Liv asks.

"I actually did."

"When?"

"About a week and a half ago."

"What?" Liv stops in her tracks, and a guy nearly plows into her. He huffs and goes around us. She ignores him. "And you didn't tell me?"

"Don't be mad. There wasn't anything to tell."

"You are so lying," she says.

We walk again, and it takes a moment to figure out exactly what I want to say and what I want to leave out, because I know she's hurt that I've been holding this in. "Okay," I say with caution, "so I came to buy new boots and—"

"You don't have new boots."

"True. I said I came to buy them, not that I actually did. And while I was here, I met him. Randomly. At Starbucks. After he pointed out that I had underwear clinging to my leg."

"What?"

I tell her the story.

Liv's laughing hard.

"Stop! It's not that funny!" I say, but I'm laughing, too.

"That's freaking hilarious! What school does he go to?"

"He's a senior at JFK."

"An older man. And he's gorgeous."

"He is."

"I love how rosy your face gets when you blush."

"Shut it, Liv!"

We wait for her mom between the double doors by Hot Topic. It's too cold to wait outside, and we left our jackets in the car so we wouldn't have to carry them through the mall.

"You know," I say, leaning on the cold glass and watching people enter and exit. "I've been thinking a lot about what you've been saying to me, how I deserve to be happy and how I should move on, and I agree."

Liv pulls me into a bear hug. "You do. And you should. But you know what, maybe I was wrong."

"About what?"

"About doing things to make Josh jealous. He isn't worth your time anymore. Maybe you should go to the dance with a guy who really seems to like you, who you could have a real relationship with. Like Hayden."

"I'm not sure. That'll make things so…real."

"What's wrong with real?"

"Real sometimes hurts."

"I know. But sometimes it doesn't."

She's probably right. I'm just so scared of being hurt again. I remember how many times Liv helped me through the bad times with Josh. Even Briana helped me then. Looking back, there were a lot of bad times with Josh. Huh. Maybe I never realized how much better off I am without him.

"I'll think about it," I say to Liv. "And thanks. You're a good friend."

She gives me a cheesy smile.

"Now I want to be one to you. Tell me about Andy."

"You already are," she says, to which I return the same smile. "And what about him?"

"Tell me why you're afraid of having a relationship." She stares at me. A couple walks out through one set of doors, so we are quiet until they proceed through the other set and into the cold air.

"I'm not afraid."

"Liv," I begin when we see her mom's headlights.

"Mom's here."

"Look Liv, I didn't mean to upset you," I say as I open the door. Brisk air slaps my cheeks. "It was just…an observation."

"I know," she says and hugs her dress to her chest. I do the same with mine, toss my empty coffee cup into a trash pail, and we get into the car.

The drive home is quiet except for Liv's mom asking about our dresses and our answers. When they drop me off, I tell Liv to text me later and she says she will. I try to read her expression, but it's too dark. But I can't let it go. As soon as I go up to my room, after I show Mom my dress and then hang it on the back of my bedroom door, I call her.

"And I really didn't mean anything by the kiss with Andy," I say when she answers.

"I know."

Is that all she's going to say? "Andy really likes you."

"He does?"

"A lot."

There's a pause on her end, and if I know my best friend, I'm willing to bet she's smiling right now.

"You're right," she blurts. "About me. I didn't think anyone noticed." She sighs. "I've never admitted this to anyone. I'm… scared of relationships."

"Scared? You?" Really, it's all I can say. I'm shocked by this. If I were to guess, I'd have said it was because she wanted to keep all the doors open. *Possibilities*, I'd heard her say before. But thinking back on it all now, she's always been so on top of me about guys and my relationships. Maybe she was living through my experiences.

"Yeah. I don't know why. I guess I'm really insecure."

More than any other possibility I've thought of before, this one takes me by surprise. Liv is no Helena. That's more my thing. "You're more of a Hermia," I say.

"Who?"

I forgot. She's not learning that in her English class. They're tackling The Great Gatsby. The novel, not the movie or TV adaptation.

I fill her in on the play. By the time I'm done, even my head's spinning.

"That's a lot of who-loves-who-who-loves-somebody-else," Liv says.

That reminds me of the old 80's song, so I sing her a few lines. "If my life had a theme song, that'd be it," I say when I'm done butchering it, and we laugh.

"But love doesn't really stink," Liv says.

"For you, too."

"Ah. Good one."

"I know."

"I'm glad you met Hayden, even if it involved a pilfered bra."

"Ha! It was humiliating."

"I bet." After a moment, she says, "I think he's good for you. I feel it."

I hope she's right. It's on the tip of my tongue to tell her everything about him and April and the phones.

I need to tell him, too. I think about what happened today. What if he really was telling the truth about April? That would mean he hadn't been deceitful. Unlike me.

So yeah, I'm going to come clean with them both. Soon.

CHAPTER NINETEEN

After Liv and I hang up, I take out my English homework. I reread my essay and add a few thoughts here and there. I stick with the Love is Blind theme and stay focused on Helena and her insecurities. I don't add much to what I've already written; I mainly edit and embellish it to bring me closer to the minimum word count of 1,000 and add thoughts on how things might be today for Helena versus how it may have been in Shakespeare's time. Back in the olden days, she'd simply have to deal—to get over herself or end up a miserly old maid. Today, she might need to see a therapist or read a self-help book.

It's late by the time I'm done, so I tuck my homework into my backpack and dress for bed. But no matter how hard I try, I can't sleep.

I keep picking up my phone, wanting to text Hayden. To tell him we need to talk. To tell him I might be ready to have a relationship. But I don't. Instead, I scoop Mooks up and hug him close. I imagine it's Hayden, and I close my eyes. What would it feel like to kiss him? I picture his warm, sweet breath on my face, his gentle hand on my chin lifting it up so my lips meet his and….

"Claire? You up?" It's Evan. He peeks in. *"Were you just kissing that monkey?"*

"What? No! What?!" I sit up fast and toss Mooks aside. "Knock next time!"

"Sorry." He's trying not to giggle. I can tell.

"What do you want?"

"I have to ask you something."

"You've got sixty seconds. Go."

Evan closes the door. And stands there.

"You're wasting your seconds."

He rests one foot on my old skateboard, pushing it back and forth. It makes a rolling sound on the hardwood. "I want to ask Leah to go out with me, but I'm not sure how."

"Evan, you're already with her," I say.

"I know, but I want to go *out* with her."

"Do you mean *out*-out? As in, *a specific place?* You already—"

"Nooo." He breathes hard through his lips. "I mean with her, as in only us. A couple."

"Ah," I say. "Going steady. That's what they used to say in ancient times. When Mom and Dad were kids."

"Exactly."

"So what's the problem?"

Evan gives me the *duh* look. "She has a ton of friends. One is a guy."

"And?"

Evan stares.

"You think she might have another boyfriend?"

He shrugs.

"I can't really help you there. You'll have to ask her that yourself."

"What if she does?"

"Then she doesn't deserve you, Evan. Don't be a doormat. Like Helena."

"Who's Helena?"

"Some chick in a Shakespeare play. Not important. What's important is you need to believe in yourself."

Evan stops swishing the skateboard with a huff, and then plops onto the edge of my bed next to me, his shoulders slumping. "It's *scary*," he says. "I don't want to ruin anything between us by asking. I mean, it's not like you and that guy at the mall. Is he the one who gave you the monkey?"

"We're just friends," I blurt. "And how did you know about that?"

He shrugs one shoulder. "I saw you together when you took me and Leah. I put two and two together. Duh. And that's a pretty cool monkey..." He points to Mooks behind me.

"Enough with the monkey!"

"Okay, okay. What I'm trying to say is, I want to be with Leah, but I'm not sure if she wants to be my girlfriend. Like, I'd be her *boyfriend*."

I want to smile at how adorable he seems right now, but I hold back so he doesn't think I'm laughing at him again.

I clear my throat. "Listen, Evan, if you want to ask her to be with only you, then ask. Be honest."

I picture Cupid on my shoulder, pointing his fat finger at me, going, "*Honesty, ha! Great advice coming from you, Claire!*"

Ignoring my snarky imagination, I focus on my brother. "Just say what you feel, but be prepared for her answer. She might say no. Would you be okay with that?"

"No," Evan says. "But if she wants to be with someone else and me at the same time, I wouldn't be okay with that, either."

"Right. So if she likes you, she'll say yes. If she doesn't, you'll have to move on."

Evan looks terrified. "But I really like her."

"I know, but it's not fair to keep stringing you along." I think about how hurt I felt over Josh. Had I asked him if he wanted to see other people, to break up, it would have hurt to hear his answer, but it would have hurt way less than finding him with Briana.

"I mean…who does she think she is?" I stand up fast. "If she wants to have boys swooning after her, fine, but what then? Leave you sitting there looking like a fool? No way!"

Evan is hanging onto my every word.

"In fact, don't ask her. Just tell her. Say, 'If you want to be with me, it has to be only me. If not, 'ciao. Sayonara. Adios, amigo.'"

"That's *amiga*," Evan corrects.

I wave my hand. "Whatever. You get my point, don't you? Be confident."

Evan stands up, taller. No more slumped shoulders. "I think so. Thanks, Claire."

"Anytime, *mi hermano*."

"And Claire?" Evan pauses by the door. "You should be with Hayden. I meant what I said before. You seem…happy when you're with him. Not like after, well, you know…."

"Yeah, I know. I'll think about it. Now, get out."

Evan leaves and closes the door. I hope I gave him the right advice. He should be confident. And he should be honest with Leah. If everyone were honest in this world, there'd be way less confusion and a lot more happiness.

I fall asleep thinking, *Now, if only I could take my own advice.*

The next day, all Liv does is obsess about what hairstyle she's going to wear at the dance, announcing more than once: "I need an appointment with your mom, *STAT!*" So first thing after ninth period, I text Mom and ask to arrange appointments for Liv and me at the salon for our dance hairstyles.

"We're booked at the salon for 1:00 on Saturday," I tell Liv on our way to decorating committee after school. "I just got a text back from my mom."

"Oh, good. Thanks," she says, and we enter the gym. Josh and Briana are at their table. Liv and I sit down at ours while we wait for Andy to show.

"So, Liv," I whisper. "Have you thought about getting together with Andy?"

Liv smiles. "Thanks to you, yes."

"Really?"

She nods.

"That's awesome, Liv. He's going to be so happy."

"Can you speak to him for me?"

"Of course I will."

"Wait until I'm not around, though."

I lean over and give her a hug. "You two will make such a cute couple," I whisper in her ear.

A few minutes later, Andy arrives, looking nervous as he runs his hands through his hair about a million times.

"Hi, Claire," he says, sitting beside me, side-eying Liv. Just then Josh walks past. For the first time since our breakup, I don't care.

"Hey, Claire," Josh says and keeps walking.

Andy must notice, because he sits straighter and comes closer to me. I give him the cut-throat sign but I think he's too nervous about Liv being a few feet from him to get my meaning. He leans over and kisses my cheek. Josh doesn't see it, but Liv does. She looks away and I feel awful.

Josh sits beside Briana. For the first time ever, I also don't mind seeing them together. They actually seem happy. Good together, even.

Maybe it wasn't meant for me to be with him. But was I meant to be friends with Briana forever? I'm not sure. But I feel there's something I need to do.

First, I lean toward Andy. "I'll be right back. Right now, I think you need to talk to Liv." We both look over. She's busying herself with a list that Madison gave her, scrutinizing it. I know for a fact that Liv could look it over and, in ten seconds, know what's what. So this is her being sad and feeling weird.

"Is she upset?" Andy asks.

"Well, let's just say she really likes you," I whisper.

Andy's whole face beams.

I hold up a finger. "But she's never had a real relationship, so…"

"Never?"

"Nope. She's scared. But she likes you."

Andy gets up and makes his way over to her. She smiles when he sits next to her, and they begin to talk.

Feeling confident that I totally helped Liv out, I get up and make my way across the gym. When I stop at their table, Josh looks up. He's wearing a shocked expression on his face. Then Briana looks up, too.

"I need to talk to you, Briana," I say before I lose my nerve.

She sighs and rolls her eyes. "Fine." She gets up, I assume for us to go somewhere private, but I stop her.

"We can talk here. It's not secret."

"Don't start any crap, Claire," Josh says.

I ignore him. Briana and I are face to face. "Briana, you were one of my best friends. I loved you. We did so much together. And I miss that. I miss you—the old you."

She starts to roll her eyes again, probably expecting me to tell her off.

"No, this isn't that," I say. "I hate what you did to me." I look at Josh for this part. "What you both did. But I want to tell you that I'm over it. I don't hate either of you anymore. I'm moving on, and I hope you're both happy."

My eyes have filled up, so before tears can fall, I turn away and head back to Liv and Andy, who are looking at me with their jaws practically on the table. It takes, like, a year and a half to get across that gym, but when I finally get to our table and sit back down, a gigantic weight rolls off my shoulders and thunks onto the shiny wooden floor.

"Not here, and not now," Liv says, trying to keep a straight face for Josh and Briana's benefit—who may or not still be here; I dare not look. "But you better tell me everything that just happened."

But then something comes over me. A calmness. "There isn't much to tell," I say and let out a long breath. "I'm moving on, that's all."

CHAPTER TWENTY

By Thursday, I still haven't called Hayden. I'm totally procrastinating because I promised myself that, when I did speak to him, I'd tell him the truth about April. I'm scared.

I'm also afraid to tell Liv, mostly because whenever I think about it, I'm embarrassed about what I did. But I know that the longer I wait, the harder it's going to be.

At the end of the day, I decide I'm going to skip the dance committee meeting. I'm just too tired. I'm sure Liv will forgive me this one time. I hardly slept at all last night. I was too busy thinking about everything: Briana and Josh, and how things used to be with each of them. How great Liv is, and how I shouldn't be holding anything back from her. The last person on the planet who'd ever hurt me is her. She deserves more than the friendship I've given her so far. Because I've been so distrusting, my vision's been skewed.

I made a vow to myself last night to not only come clean, but to trust more. That one's going to be hard.

I'm engrossed with all of these thoughts as I walk toward the buses, so I don't see the person in front of me until I walk into them.

"Sorry, I—" I look up past the denim jacket and find a face... *Josh's* face.

"Oh. It's you." I try to step around him, but he blocks me.

"Wait," he says.

Did he step in front of me so I'd bump into him?

I clear my throat. "What's up?"

"Hello to you, too." Josh tries to smile, but I can see it's forced, maybe a little awkward.

I don't falter. I just wait for the answer to my question by raising one eyebrow as people are forced to walk around us.

"I've, uh, been meaning to talk to you."

"About what." It's a question that comes out like a statement. After all these weeks, I thought that talking to him would make me a blubbery mess. But there's a new strength that's coming out of me right now, one I never knew I had.

"Nothing specific." He studies me. "You seem...different."

"Different how?"

He shrugs. "Can't put my finger on it. Just different. I like it."

I'm not sure how to answer that, so I don't.

"I miss you."

I blink. "Really, Josh? You're with Briana, remember? Or are you trying to cheat on her, too? Because if you are, I'm not the one you should be talking to."

"Aw, come on, Claire. Don't be like that. I'm just talking to you."

"No, you're not. This conversation's over."

"Okay then, bye." He winks at me. Then he leaves me standing there, stumped.

I take a window seat on my bus and plunk down, fingers flying as I text Liv about what just happened.

She answers in one second flat: **What a jerk!!**

We go back and forth, calling Josh every name we could come up with, even the gross ones, until we're both laughing.

I'm coming home, she texts. **Not much going on here**

anyway. Andy had an art thing to do for one of his teachers. Meet you at my house?

I think it over. It actually sounds great. I tell her I'll be there, and she and her mom pull into their driveway at the same time I arrive. We bump fists and head to her room after she makes popcorn and fills two bowls.

"So much happened today," she says.

"I know, right?"

I tell her all about Josh and Briana.

"I'm so proud of you for telling them both how you feel," Liv says. She squeezes my arm. "I knew you had this. It was just a matter of time."

"Thanks, Liv." I'm too tired to tell her anything more. And why ruin the moment by telling her how dumb I was to pretend to be another girl? I'll save it for another time.

"So now what?" Liv asks.

"Netflix?"

"*Zombified!*" she says, reaching for her controller. She pulls it up, we get comfy stacking pillows, she makes more popcorn, and when she comes back, she presses *play*. It's time to forget everything for a while.

WHEN I GET HOME, even though it's almost 8:00 P.M. the scent of Mexican food wafts from the kitchen. Normally, I'd be all over this. But tonight, I have no appetite after all the popcorn Liv and I ate.

Mom and Dad are cooking beans & rice *con pollo* dishes. Mom looks up from the stove to greet me while Dad tastes something from a frying pan. It burns his lip, and he winces.

"Hi, honey. How was your day?" Mom asks, handing Dad a cup of cold water.

"Good."

Dad offers me a taste on a wooden spoon, after blowing on it to cool it off.

"Mm, good," I say between chews. It doesn't want to go down.

"It's almost ready," he says. "Ten more minutes."

I swallow finally. "I had a big lunch and then ate way too much popcorn at Liv's, so I'll skip dinner, okay?"

"If you're hungry later, there will be plenty," says Mom.

"How was work?" I ask them both.

"The salon's picking up," Mom says. "And Dad sold a house today." Mom smiles and hugs him from behind.

"Almost," Dad corrects. "It's under contract."

"Awesome. The Landry house?" I ask, hopeful.

"No, another one," he says. "But that one's still in the works."

"Well, congrats," I say. "To both of you."

After I grab a bottle of water, I go upstairs to my room. I'm contemplating calling Hayden. I think it's time. But before I can pull up his number, my bedroom door flies open and slams against the wall. It makes me jump.

"Hey! I told you to knock!" I say to Evan, who's standing in my doorway, arms folded across his NY Giants jersey. He's frowning. "What's with you?"

"It's your fault!" he spews at me.

"What's my fault?"

"I told Leah what you said, and you know what she did? She broke up with me!"

His eyes are glassy. I've never seen him this angry. I don't know what to say except, "Oh, wow, Evan, I'm sorry. I didn't mean for that to happen. I swear."

"Well, it did! And now she's mad at me and will never talk to me again. She called me a control freak!"

"Because you said you wanted to be a couple? That's not very fair."

"No, because I told her the way you said to. That if she

couldn't be with only me, then goodbye. And she said it made me sound bossy and made her sound like she's easy."

"*Easy?* She said that?"

"Yeah. She said she's never had a boyfriend before me, and she's not interested in anyone else. She freaked out and was crying, Claire. Crying!"

"I'm so sorry, I—"

Evan slams the door in my face.

I try all night to coax Evan into talking to me. He refuses to give in. So I give up. Dinner is long over with, and I still have no appetite, so I decide to go to bed. I grab Mooks and hug him tight.

"Why is love so complicated, Mooksie?" I ask him. "Not only have I turned my own love life into a boatload of poo, now Evan's is, too, and he's right—it's all my fault."

I played Cupid, but instead of shooting arrows into their hearts to induce love, I shot an anti-love potion straight into their butts.

CHAPTER TWENTY-ONE

On Friday, Evan still isn't speaking to me. Unless you count: "Get out", "Leave me alone", and "I'm not talking to you" to which I lightheartedly replied that, technically, he *was* talking to me, even if it was to tell me he wasn't, but this only resulted in another slammed door in my face.

Even after I offered to clean his room for two whole weeks, he's still not saying a word to me.

During school today, I've asked myself: *'What would Cupid do?'* a thousand times, trying to figure out how to correct the mess I helped make with my brother's love life. My answers were: A) I had no right to tell him to be so mean to Leah, B) I almost messed up Liv and Andy's relationship before it even started so who was I to butt in, and C) *Hello?* My own love life sucks! Which brings me to only one answer: Cupid would make things right.

I decide that I'm going to find out where Leah lives. I'll go to her house after school today and talk to her face-to-face. I'll explain that it was my fault, my advice, and that Evan would never have said those things without my interference. I'll beg her forgiveness, and then I'll tell her that he really likes her. Yup, that's what I'm going to do. I Google her name and find her address in about five seconds. Thank you, Internet.

I'm honestly surprised the day's not filled with fireballs shooting from the sky or random unlucky happenings, since it is Friday the thirteenth. Actually, it's been mostly uneventful. Some might consider that lucky, and I rethink my preconceived notions about the day being unlucky when, during English, Ms. Levine says she's giving us a few extra days to finish our paper since tomorrow is the dance and all. Nice.

At the end of the day, I meet Liv and Andy at the gym for our last decoration committee meeting, the one where we actually decorate. I explain that I'm only staying for half an hour so I can help my brother with something important. That's when the middle school lets out, so Leah should be home shortly after that.

Madison hands out boxes of cut-out shapes, heavy-duty tape, disco balls, and various Valentine's Day dance-themed items, and we get to work. After about twenty minutes, my second cell phone rings. I see that it's Hayden. *Shoot! I never called him back!*

I take my phone to a corner of the gym where there's the least noise, and answer the call. "Hello?"

"Hey," he says. I love the sound of his voice. "Are you free right now?"

"Not exactly. I'm still at school. Decoration committee, for tomorrow's dance."

"Can you get out early? I want to take you somewhere. It's a surprise."

"Well, I am leaving early anyway, but I have something I need to do when I leave here. I have to go to my brother's girlfriend's house and straighten something out."

"Can I take you there?"

I can't avoid seeing Hayden. I don't even want to. The sound of his voice causes goosebumps to pop up on my arms. I do want to see him. And I have to tell him. It's time.

"Sure, I'd love to hang out. And I want to talk to you about something."

"Everything all right?"

"I hope so."

"Should I worry?"

"No worries."

"Awesome." I hear the smile in his voice. "I'll pick you up at the school in, what, half an hour?"

"Perfect."

After we hang up, I float past balloons and dangly hearts and red and white streamers, which are all going up at lightning speed, and find Liv and Andy. Liv's on a ladder, hanging a giant bow and arrow high up on the wall, and Andy's "helping" her by holding the small of her back. When he sees me, he waggles his eyebrows and tips his head toward Liv.

"Listen, you guys," I say, after half an hour and after we've made a lot of headway. "I've got to bounce. Evan needs my help."

Andy steps closer to me with a look of concern on his face. Liv turns and takes two steps down from the ladder. "Is everything okay?" she asks.

"I kind of screwed up and gave him lame advice about his girlfriend. It's a long story, but he's really mad, and he's not talking to me. I have to speak to Leah and fix this."

Liv pouts. "Want me to come with?"

"That's okay. Hayden's picking me up."

Liv smiles. "Call me later. And if you need me, call sooner."

Andy nods. "Same here."

Wow, they rock. "Thanks, guys." I blow a kiss to them and head out fast to meet Hayden. As I walk down the hall toward the front doors, a swarm of bees buzz in my belly.

I call Mom to tell her I'm going out with Hayden. By the time I hang up with her, I'm at the front doors of the school. It's chilly out, so I zip my jacket all the way up to my chin and step outside to wait for Hayden.

I'm not waiting long when I hear Josh's voice.

"Claire?"

I turn around. "I'm not in the mood for this right now, Josh."

He holds up a hand. "Just hear me out. I don't like the way we left things off the other day. I just want to say I'm sorry. Okay? I can't deal if you hate me."

There's a bunch of things I can say to that, but I refrain. It'll come out as sarcastic and mean, so I swallow the words.

"I don't hate you," I say. He doesn't deserve my kindness, but I'm not cruel.

"Good." He smiles a little. "So...are you with that guy?"

It takes me a moment to realize who he means. "Oh, Andy? No. We're not together. He's more Liv's type."

"Cool."

Just then, Hayden pulls up to the curb.

"I have to go," I say. I rush away before Josh can say another thing, and I hop into Hayden's jeep, the kind where the doors and roof come off and there are roll bars. I don't look back to see if Josh is still standing there. Instead, I focus on Hayden's car.

"Nice ride," I say, trying to keep my voice even.

"Thanks. Who was that?"

My stomach twists for a moment. I feel guilty even though nothing happened. "My ex."

Hayden looks over to where Josh was. I look, too, as I buckle my seatbelt, relieved he's no longer standing there.

"It was nothing," I say fast.

"Nothing?" He's gripping the steering wheel tightly.

"Trust me." For a second, I want to take those words back. But I don't.

He loosens his grip on the wheel and smiles a bit. Then we pull away from the curb.

"So where are we going?" I ask, glad to change the subject.

"I think we need to stop at your house to get you a warmer jacket. And maybe gloves."

"Why? Are we going on an Alaskan nature walk?"

"I told you, it's a surprise. So...remind me how to get there."

I show him the way to my house, and while he drives, he seems bothered by something.

"So, Claire, what did you want to talk to me about?"

Oh. That.

I don't know how to tell him. I need to know if he likes April that way, too. I bring that up first. "That girl. The one who you were talking to on Tuesday."

"April?"

"Yeah. Her."

The corners of his mouth curve. Is he laughing at me being jealous?

"What about her?"

"Is she...do you...I mean..."

"Is she someone I'm interested in? No. Is she someone my friend is interested in? Very much so."

"Oh." I lean back in my seat. Stare at him. Is he telling me the truth?

He must sense my thoughts. He turns to me fast and then looks back at the road. "You've got it all wrong, Claire. I met her at my friend, Mark's. He's into her, not me." I let him explain the rest, trying not to judge. "He had this party," he continues. "Well, he actually had two parties this month. His parents go away a lot on weekends. Anyway, a few weeks ago, she was at his house. He felt too weird around her, so he asked me to talk to her for him. I know. That was real immature, right?" He laughs a little, and I do, too, but really what would he think of all the things I've done if he thinks *that* was immature?

"We hit it off as friends, you know? She was really nice, and Mark deserves to be with someone like her. He's had it rough. Bad break up."

I nod, totally understanding the feeling.

"She'd just broken up with her boyfriend though, so she was

being cautious. We talked about that and about a lot of other stuff. Talking came easy for the both of us. I told her I'd be there to talk any time. She said she liked Mark, too, but wanted to take things slowly. I gave her my number, she wrote hers on a napkin. I must've called the wrong number by mistake because that day I met you? I was supposed to meet her to see if she wanted to get to know Mark better. I said I'd help her with that. But she never showed. Later on, she told me she'd never gotten my message."

But I got that message instead.

He looks over and smiles at me. "But then I met you." My whole body warns.

"The strange thing was, though, that someone did answer my message. I've been talking to someone who's been answering my texts. This whole time I thought it was her. It wasn't. Who could do something like that? It's a low-life thing to do."

I'm dying a little. I loosen my scarf from around my neck.

"Want me to turn down the heat?"

He does, and I stare out the window. There's no way I can tell him now. No way at all. This is going to have to be my secret from now on. Forever and ever.

CHAPTER TWENTY-TWO

We pull up in front of my house a few minutes later. I've composed myself enough to know I cannot tell him about April. Nope. No way. Not happening. I decide that from here on out, I'll continue to act as though our relationship really had started with a random meeting. Hayden isn't into April, and what a relief that is to me.

When we enter the house, Mom is at it again with the interrogation, even though we've been through this already, the last time she met him. I give her "the gesture" behind his back, waving my arms, but she ignores me and asks Hayden a million questions anyway.

Sigh.

"So, Hayden, where are you from?" she asks.

"Bloomington," he says.

"What do your parents do?"

"Really, Mom?" I say, but Mom continues to ignore me and Hayden's too polite not to answer.

"My mom's an ER nurse, and my dad's a bank exec."

"Nice. How long have you been working at the mall?" she asks.

"About a year now," he says. "I'm taking photography in school and hope to be a professional photographer one day."

"Great." Mom persists. "Is that your jeep?"

"Yeah, I just got it. Saved up all year."

Mom nods, impressed. "A practical boy."

I'm *practically* dying behind him, waving my arms, trying to get her to stop. Finally, *thankfully*, she does. Thank goodness Dad's not here, or Hayden would have been tied to a chair with a huge, hanging light in his face.

I grab a heavier coat from the hall closet. "You might want gloves, too," Hayden says. "It's getting colder out."

"Where are you two off to?" Mom asks. I listen for the answer, but he whispers it to Mom, and when he pulls back from her, she smiles and nods. Normally I'd be so giddy over this kind of thing. I mean, I'm happy being around Hayden no matter where he takes me. And on a normal day, the adorable surprise of today's date would make my stomach do a jig with my heart. But right now, all I can think about is my lie and how Hayden felt about a person pretending to be someone else.

"Nice. Have fun," Mom says, breaking my thoughts. "And be careful driving, please."

"Always," Hayden says. We head down the driveway.

"Seatbelts!" she calls, making me flinch. "Have Claire back before too late!"

"I'll have her back before nine, Mrs. Parker. And I'll have her text you my cell number."

Through the passenger window, I give Mom a final look, one that begs for her not to interrogate him any further.

"I'm sorry," I say to him once we pull away. *For lying. For pretending to be April. For not being the person you think I am.*

"It's cool. My mom's the same way." He pulls out of my drive-way, and we start down the street. "Where to?"

I show him the way to Leah's house. If I can't make things

right with Hayden, maybe I can with my brother. I just hope I don't make things worse.

CHAPTER TWENTY-THREE

BY THE TIME we get there, I know Leah's home already, because it's now almost 3:20, thanks to Mom's tiresome questions. I knock on the door, and Leah answers. At first, she seems confused. "Hi, Claire. What are you doing here?" She pokes her head out the door farther, I assume to look for Evan.

"Hey, Leah. No, Evan's not here. It's just me. That's Hayden." I point with my thumb at Hayden in the jeep. He waves, so she waves, too, before looking back at me. "Sorry to bug you," I say. "Can we talk for a minute?"

"Sure." Her eyebrows are still furrowed, but she calls over her shoulder to her mom to tell her she'll be outside. Then she reaches for her jacket and slips it on before coming outside.

"So," I begin, "I came to apologize to you."

"To me? For what?"

"Because you guys broke up and it's all my fault." Leah looks intrigued, but says nothing. I continue, "See, I had this boyfriend, and he cheated on me. It really sucked. It was the worst day of my life and I—"

"Really? Oh my gosh, Claire, are you okay? What happened?"

This is not going the way I'd planned. Time to re-route. Focus.

"Yeah, yeah, I'm fine. But this isn't about me; it's about you. And Evan."

"Huh?"

I take a breath and begin again. "Listen, I gave Evan crappy advice. I told him what to say to you the other day, about being with him only or *adios.*"

Her expression changes to *Oh. Now I'm pissed.*

"Yeah, so...he came to me for advice because he really likes you and he wasn't sure how to ask you to be exclusive with him. You know, to be a couple. But when he mentioned you had friends who are boys, I guess I took things too far because I was feeling pretty bitter myself. Anyway, I must've put things in his head, and he got jealous. Does that make sense?"

Leah's lips form a small smile. "He was jealous?"

"Yeah."

"And worried that I wouldn't like him anymore?"

"Uh-huh. And now he's a big mess."

"Hmm."

I'm not sure what she means by that, but she smiles, so I take the cue and keep going. "See, Evan's not normally like that. He's never had a girlfriend before."

"Aw, really?"

Uh-oh. If this gets back to him, Evan's going to kill me. I bite the inside of my cheek to keep more stuff from spewing out.

"That's so sweet," Leah says, twirling her hair around her pointer finger.

"Well...I'm just here to ask you to please forgive him, and if you're going to be mad at someone, be mad at me. It wasn't his fault. Not at all."

She ponders this for a few excruciating moments. *Twirling, twirling, twirling.* If this were an old-timey soap opera on TV right before a commercial, the announcer would ask: "Will Leah forgive Evan? Will she run to him and tell him off despite Claire's efforts? Will she tell him how lame Claire made him sound? Will Evan forgive Claire for meddling?"

"You know, I've never had a boyfriend before either," Leah says, zapping me back into reality.

"So I guess you two are made for each other then." I give her a wide smile.

"Hey. Yeah," she says mid-twirl. "Thanks *so much* for coming over to explain this to me."

"No problem. So you're good with Evan?"

"Sure."

"Great. Well, bye." I waggle my fingers in a wave and step off her front porch.

"Thanks again, Claire," she calls to me.

I turn around just as the front door closes. "Just call me Cupid," I say to myself. Then I let out a long breath.

I hop back into the jeep, and twenty minutes later, we arrive in Port Mathers, a small harbor town with shops and restaurants and a small beach area with picnic tables. My family has spent many summer days here, walking along the water's edge, watching small boats and yachts pulling in and out of the harbor. But now, in winter, it's kind of desolate.

"I've never been here this time of year," I say, looking around.

Hayden pulls around to the Town Center building, a big red structure that resembles a barn, and slips into a parking spot. He turns off the engine, and it gets super quiet. "Ready?"

"I guess?"

Inside the building, it's warm and a polite middle-aged woman greets us. Hayden leans over the counter and whispers something to her. She points, and Hayden guides me to a window, where an older man is on the other side. "Hello. What size?" the guy asks me.

"Huh?"

"What size shoe do you wear?" Hayden asks. I've been asked

many strange things in my lifetime, but this is one for the records. When I don't answer, Hayden says, "We're going ice skating."

"Ice skating?" I repeat. "Really? I always wanted to go ice skating."

"Well, then I'm glad."

"Is there a rink here?" I look around, but see only a large room in the center and offices off to the side.

The guy behind the window seems unamused. "Of course we have one," he interrupts, "or we wouldn't be handing out ice skates. So…what's your size?"

I tell him and gleefully hand him my Vans in exchange for a pair of brown skates. One blade.

"Do you want to try two blades first?" Hayden asks as he's handed a pair of his own.

"No. I want to live dangerously."

I love Hayden's smile.

He laces my skates for me and then shakily guides me one teeny, slippery step at a time toward the rink opening. Walking on skates is a whole lot different—and easier—than skating on skates. The rink is small, but it's outside and there are only a few other skaters out here with us: a mom and two small kids and an older couple about my grandparents' age. The couple is so cute, holding hands. I admire how, every time the woman is shaky, the man steadies her and vice versa.

Hayden guides me on the ice, when I'm not clinging to the railing, and he shows me how to keep my ankles straight. But I feel like I've forgotten how to use my legs and feet. And I seem to have zero balance. Each time one of my feet slides forward, my other foot slips from behind, making me wobble and fall onto my butt. This happens about a bazillion times, and I can't help but laugh every time I land, which is about every two-point-three seconds. By tomorrow, my butt will be black and blue for sure, but somehow, I don't care.

"This is the most fun I've had in so long!" I tell Hayden while he pulls me along by holding both of my hands and skating backwards. I'm unsteady, which makes me laugh and then I teeter even more.

Hayden lets go of my hands. I yelp. "Ah! Help!"

"You've got it!"

"No, I don't!" My arms flail like propellers.

"Steady!" he says. He reaches for me and goes for my hands, but I'm too busy trying not to fall forward. Which I do anyway, and in the process Hayden falls backwards.

I scream and laugh at the same time, putting my hands out in front of me to break my fall, but I don't have to, because I land smack on top of him.

"Are...you...okay?" he says. I can feel his body beneath mine, shaking from laughter.

"Me?" I say through my own laughter. "I fell on you! Are *you* okay?"

Hayden's expression gets serious, and his eyes lock with mine. "Never been better."

I suck in my breath. Cold air fills my lungs, but I'm warm all over. Our faces are an inch apart. He pulls me toward him. Our lips come closer together.

"Are you two all right?" a voice says, causing us both to look up with a start.

Hayden gets up first and then he helps me to my wobbly feet. I brush the ice shavings off my coat and pants while still clinging to Hayden's arm.

"We're good," Hayden says to the kind elderly man, whose wife skates over and stops beside him.

"You took some spill," the man says and pats Hayden on the back. "Glad you're both okay. Carry on." He snaps off a military-style salute and begins to lead the woman away, but not before she leans over to me and says, "You make an adorable couple." I feel myself blush. "I know a good match when I see one." She lifts her hand, which is holding her husband's, and together they skate away.

"That was weird," I say, feeling a bit embarrassed and unsure of what to say.

"I thought it was awesome," Hayden says. "She must be clairvoyant. Oh, hey—"

"I know, I know, I'm *Claire-voyant*, too. My brother says that to me all the time."

"Maybe it's a sign," he says with a grin. "Come." He pulls me slowly, and after a few more minutes, we're gliding more gracefully on the ice.

The elderly couple is holding hands, skating ahead of us. "I hope to be like them one day," Hayden says, his voice wistful.

"Good skaters?" I ask, knowing full well what he meant. He means in love. Together. Having that special something, a connection, that two people can share forever.

"That and they're spiffy dressers," he teases.

We skate a few more times around the rink and stop at an opening along the railing. "Are we ready to go?" he asks after the third time. "Have we had enough skating for one day?"

I rub my achy backside with my other hand. "I think my butt will thank me to leave."

Hayden playfully leans behind me and cups a hand around his mouth. "You hear that?" he says to my butt, which is weird but hilarious at the same time. "We're going to leave now. You can relax!"

Laughing, we trade in our skates and retrieve our shoes—and feel *really short* once we're back in them. And have I forgotten how to walk? I check in with a quick text to Mom, and then Hayden takes me home. All the way back, as we listen to one of his punk-rock mix playlists, I relive every minute of tonight: how I fell a million times, and how patient he was when teaching me, and how, when we both fell, we were *so close* to kissing.

We reach my house too soon. "Thanks," I say. "I had a great time."

"Perfect." Hayden leans over the bucket seats. I lean in too and close my eyes. And he kisses me—on the cheek. A short peck. I'm disappointed, but I know he's moving slowly, so I appreciate that. And I don't want to spoil today, so I straighten my shoulders and hop out of the car.

"'Night," he says.

"'Night." I close the jeep's door and float toward the house. My legs feel all rubbery, as if I'm still skating. I hope I'm not walking funny.

Once inside, I peek out the door and watch him pull away. I hug myself and sigh. It really was a perfect day, even though it was Friday the thirteenth and even *without* a kiss-kiss. But that quickly changes when I turn around and see Evan.

And he's glaring at me.

CHAPTER TWENTY-FOUR

"Why?" Evan's stare sends chills down my entire body and back up again. "You had to butt in, didn't you?"

I know he means Leah. I bet she called him. "I was only trying to help. You were so ma—"

"CUTE!" he says, cutting me off. "She thinks I'm *cute*!"

"And this is bad because…?"

Evan takes a few steps toward me and points. "You know exactly why it's bad."

I shrug and wince at the same time. "Enlighten me?"

Evan huffs. "She's got all her friends ooh-ing and ahh-ing about me all over the Internet. The Internet! She posted a picture of me on Instagram with the caption, 'My cutesie, cuddly, pookie-bear Evan. Hashtag LUVBUG.'"

I bite my lip. *Don't laugh, don't laugh, don't laugh…*

"*Love bug*. And *pookie bear*, Claire!"

"Hey, you're a poet and you don't even know it." I smile with my teeth, trying to lighten the mood and ignoring the memory this brings back of Hayden, but Evan sulks and folds his arms across his chest.

"Not funny."

"Well," I say with a shaky voice because I still want to laugh, and I'm not sure if it's because this whole thing's kind of funny or that he's making me nervous. "At least she called you a bear. It's better than being called, I don't know, a chicken." I burst out laughing. I can't help it.

"How is this funny to you?"

"Come on, Evan, look on the bright side," I say. "Didn't you get back together with her?"

"Well, yeah, but now she's never going to take me seriously. She wants to take me with her to get a manicure and pedicure. Then I'm sure she'll post pictures of that, too. What'll those captions say? 'Evan's pretty in pink?'"

This makes me laugh harder as I picture my brother sitting in a salon, having his nails done in *Frilly Fuchsia*.

Dad comes out of the kitchen. "What's funny?" he says.

"I'm an Internet meme!" Evan says.

"I don't even know what that means, but it sounds hilarious," Dad says, and he joins me laughing.

I can see Evan's fighting laughter, too, but he tries to stay angry as he pulls the picture up on his phone to show us. It's even funnier seeing it in person. Soon, he's full-out laughing with us.

"An Internet meme!" I say. "Maybe you'll go viral like Grumpy Cat."

"Ah," says Dad. "Now I get it." I shake my head at Dad's slowness.

"I guess it's not that bad," Evan eventually says and slips his phone back into his pocket. "At least she thinks I'm sensitive."

"Exactly," I tell him. "Girls love that."

"They certainly do," Dad says. "Oh, by the way, dinner's in the fridge, Claire Bear. I made chicken."

"Chicken!" Evan and I say at the same time, and now we're laughing all over again. This time we don't explain anything to Dad. It's our little secret.

.   .   .

"PROJECT JEALOUSY IS WELL UNDERWAY." Andy's voice is on the other end of my cell phone. His call has just awakened me, pulling me from a blissful dream where Hayden and I were on a deserted island with nothing but chocolate bars, cheese, and mocha lattes for food and drink and not one other person around.

"What? Andy, why are you calling me at…" I squint at my alarm clock and lean up on my pillow. "8:30 *on a Saturday morning?*"

"Sorry. I'm just really excited."

"Why's that?"

"Liv's so jealous. I had an idea with our plan, so I texted her and told her I changed my mind about the dance, you know, about going with her? I told her I wanted to take you instead. So she said that you and I would have a better time without her and she wasn't going at all. Isn't that cool?"

I sit straight up in bed. I forgot to tell him Project Jealousy was off! "She what?"

"I don't understand. So this isn't good?"

"No, it is not!"

I leap out of bed and sift through the pile of clean and mostly-clean clothes on my bedroom floor. I find yesterday's jeans. Good enough. I slip them on, hopping on one foot and then the other while balancing the phone between my jaw and shoulder.

"The plan is off, and I forgot to tell you," I say, rummaging for a t-shirt that I find and change into. "I had words with Josh and even Briana. Then Liv and I talked, and we both decided making him jealous isn't worth it, and we talked about you, and I told her that you liked her, and she said she liked you, too, and I said she should be in a relationship with you because she deserves to be and she was all for it, and oh my gosh, she must think I was lying to her!"

"Maybe it's not so good that I told her 'okay, sure' then, huh?"

"Oh no. Tell me you didn't."

Andy's quiet on the other end. "Do you think she's mad at me?" he finally says.

"Probably."

"Great. I screwed up."

I sigh. "No, it was my fault. This is what I get for playing Cupid. I'll call her." I search my room for my left sneaker. "I'm sorry. I keep messing things up."

"We all make mistakes," Andy says. "And, for the record, I'm glad you feel that way about Josh now. You're too good for him."

"Thanks," I say.

"I hope I haven't ruined my chances with Liv."

"I'll talk to her." I brush the tangles out of my hair and throw it into a low ponytail. "I'll go and see her now, okay? You said that she texted you this morning, right?"

"Yeah. About half an hour ago."

"Then she's up. I'll text you after I talk to her."

"Good luck. You're probably going to need it."

I LEAVE A NOTE FOR EVAN, who's still sleeping. Mom always works on Saturdays, and Dad went into the office to deal with some paperwork this morning. I hop on my bike and pedal to Liv's. I'm unsure what to expect, but when I get there, I'm out of breath and my heart's racing, and I know it's not just from the bike ride.

Liv's little brother, Manny, lets me in. I try not to laugh at his bedhead. He literally has hair standing in about twenty different directions. I say a quick hello to him and then another to her parents when I pass them in the kitchen and get a whiff of the bacon that's frying. I climb the steps to Liv's room and stand at the door, take a breath to calm me, and knock twice.

"Yeah." She sounds pretty down.

I open the door a crack and peek in. "Liv? It's me. Can I come in?"

"You're halfway there already, so…."

I can tell this isn't going to be easy. I carefully step inside and close the door behind me. The soft click it makes is amplified in the quiet of her room.

Liv's sitting cross-legged on her bed and has an open magazine in her lap, which she is looking down at, even though I'm standing there.

"Are you okay?"

Now she looks up at me. Are her eyes red and puffy from crying, or just because she just woke up not too long ago? "What, did Andy call you?"

"Actually, he did."

"Oh. Of course he did." She purses her lips. Looks down at the magazine again and flips through a few pages, hard.

"Liv, I wasn't lying to you. I don't like—"

She stops and looks up again. "Don't."

Her abruptness takes me by surprise. "Don't what?" She's never been mad at me before. I can't say I'm not uneasy.

"Don't explain anything," she says. "I'm not sure I want to hear it. And we've spoken about it before, so I already know what you're going to say."

"Liv, I forgot to tell Andy that the jealousy thing was off. I totally forgot to talk to him at all!"

"You forgot? You said you would talk to him for me. But I never said you could tell him I never had a real boyfriend!"

Oh, no.

"You told him that I'm afraid to be in a relationship! Do you know how humiliating that was?"

I swallow the huge lump in my throat. "I-I thought I was helping."

Liv's face turns pink as she goes back to the magazine flipping pages forcefully.

"You're right. I shouldn't have meddled."

"I made a fool out of myself by telling Andy it bothered me

about you and him, too. I've never made myself look vulnerable in front of a guy like that before." She sniffles, so I know she must be crying.

I stand there a moment, not knowing what to say next. Actually, I do know what to say, so I tell her exactly how I feel. It's all I can do, or I'll lose her friendship forever. Nothing is worth losing that.

"That's just it. I think that's amazing, Liv."

"Making a fool of myself?"

"No, being honest with your feelings and showing him you care, that's what's amazing to me and it's probably amazing to him, too."

She shoots me another look. "Who are you to talk about being honest?"

Ouch.

"You're right. I deserve that. But I am trying, Liv." Except am I really, if I haven't told either her or Hayden about April?

"I can't risk losing you as a friend," I say, choking up.

Liv bites the inside of her cheek.

It's time to tell her the entire truth. "But there is something else you don't know," I continue. "Well, more than one thing."

"Oh really," she says, glaring up at me. Sheesh. This isn't going to be easy.

"So, first, as I told you, Andy likes you. A lot."

"And?"

"*And*…I didn't tell him *everything* about you."

Liv contemplates this and then nods. "Okay."

"The thing is, I'd never hurt you on purpose, Liv."

"Well, thanks for *that* much."

I let the sarcasm go because I deserve that, too. "But since I knew you liked him, too," I continue, "I thought I was doing the right thing. I wanted to help get you two together. And it worked. Until he thought Project Jealousy was still happening, and he did things on his own."

"Project Jealousy?"

I sit beside her on the bed now and explain everything to her, about how it began with making Josh jealous, and then how it developed into making *her* jealous for her own good, and then about how it even spilled over to my brother's relationship, and then I didn't care to make Josh jealous anymore, and then she told me she liked Andy, so there didn't need to be anything like this going on about *her* anymore, but then I forgot to tell Andy that things were off because I'm a big, fat loser friend and I suck.

Liv shrugs. "I guess it makes sense, now that you've explained things."

I take a deep breath. "Liv, there's this other thing I haven't told you about."

Liv closes the magazine. I take another huge breath and then tell her every single thing about Hayden. I begin with the random phone call, the one I told her about that day, but never elaborated on. Then I tell her about that first trip to the mall, including April and having two phones.

"You've been pretending to be this girl?" she says. "How could you do that? And you bought a new phone? God, Claire, that's so...creepy."

"Yeah, I know, it just happened. He only met her once, at a party, and when he called me, he sounded so cute. And then after I saw him in person and actually met him, I knew I had to stay in touch with him somehow. But he'd recognize my cell number, so I had to get a new one. I had no choice."

"Who *are* you?" Liv asks.

"I'm sorry I never told you. But...there's more." I tell her about Mooks, ice-skating and the older couple and about Hayden's and my almost-kiss. When I'm done, I say, "I'm sorry I never told you all of this, Liv. I wasn't ready to tell anyone. You were right that I had to move on. And I am, but I wanted to do this alone. To see if Hayden meant something to me. And he does. I just thought that if you knew about him, you'd be all over me to make a move. I wasn't ready. I guess playing Cupid was easier because it never involved me. Trouble is I've made a few messes."

"Just a few."

"Forgive me?"

"I guess, yeah." She nudges me playfully.

"Thanks. I wasn't myself."

"You were some girl named April apparently."

It feels good to see her laughing again.

"This is so pathetic and romantic at the same time," she says after a few moments.

"I guess that makes me pretty pathetic, huh?" I say.

Liv's face softens to less angry and more sympathetic. "No. It's just wrong. You have to come clean."

"Do you think I'm messed up now?" I ask. "All this lying. Saying it all out loud this way makes it seem so wrong."

"Well, maybe just the *buying the new phone* thing is a little over the top."

"Yeah, just a little."

"Do you think Hayden will be cool with you after you tell him the truth?"

My leg bops up and down nervously. "I hope so."

"Me too." Liv stands up and holds out her hand. I take it and she helps me to my feet and gives me a hug.

"Thanks, Liv," I mumble into her shoulder.

"You're welcome," she says, squeezing me harder.

"I should go and talk to Hayden."

"Good luck. I'm going to talk to Andy."

"Good luck to you, too." I pull my jacket on. "I'll see you in a couple of hours to get our hair done for tonight, right?"

"Sure. I'll ask my mom to give us a ride to the salon."

"Great," I say, super relieved we're good now. "Well, off I go. To talk to Hayden…to come clean." I slowly head for the door but stop and turn around, about to ask her something random, when she stops me.

"Quit stalling," she says.

"You know me too well."

"You can do it, Claire."

"Thanks." But somehow, I don't think I can.

The entire time I'm pedaling my bike home, I go over the conversation I'm about to have with Hayden. I try a dozen ways to tell him what I've done. How he called me by mistake, and why I haven't told him the truth, or how I've pretended to be April.

But no matter how I spin the words and how many different ways I explain it, it still sounds bad. Like I'm a terrible person.

Because I am.

CHAPTER TWENTY-FIVE

I CAN'T DO IT.

I try over ten times to call Hayden. I press the first six numbers and as soon as I get to the seventh, I freeze. Over and over I attempt this, and each time, I hang up instead. I can't help but think about what he said, about how low the person was who did that. I keep thinking about how he's going to hate me for pretending to be someone I'm not, for making him look like a fool. He'll see me as a liar and a fake—a fake who doesn't deserve him, or anyone.

I know I should be doing this in person. Face to face. Face the music and all that. But if I see his disappointment in me once I tell him, I'll just die. So I take the cowardly route—or I will, if I can manage to make the call.

I know what'll happen. First there'll be an excruciating silence. Then he'll freak out and tell me he never wants to see me again. He'll tell me that he could never trust me. Then he'll tell me to have a nice life and hang up. And I'll feel even more devastated than when Josh and I broke up.

Because when Josh and I broke up, I felt bad for myself. We were together for all the wrong reasons. We didn't gel. I see that now. With Hayden, everything's different. We talk. We listen to each other. We care about each other's feelings. We get along. We laugh. We share a love of monkeys. It's all those things wrapped up in a ball and more.

I put the phone on the dresser and toss myself belly-first onto the bed. I grab Mooks on the way and nestle him under my chin, feeling for his two hearts, the ones that represented Hayden and me. "What am I going to do, Mooks?" I whisper. "I'm about to ruin the best thing that's ever happened to me. I wish you could talk so you could tell me what to say." I pull him away and glance at his face. Of course, he stares blankly at me, so I go back to cuddling him. And even though I would rather ignore this whole thing, pretend it isn't happening, I know I have to do this.

I reach for my phone—my real phone—and, this time, despite my shaky hand, I push all seven numbers.

Hayden picks up after the first ring. "Hey, yeah, so I know this isn't April. Get a life, dude."

I clear my throat. Swallow the snowball-sized lump in it. "Wait! Don't hang up. It's me. Claire."

"Claire?" He pauses, and I can picture him looking at his phone screen, checking the caller ID number. "I-I'm confused. This is *Claire*?"

I squeeze my eyes shut. "Yeah. We have to talk," I say almost in a whisper.

"I don't understand."

I jump in feet first. "The thing is, you called April and left a message and asked her to meet you at the mall, but you actually called me by mistake. At this number. I thought that maybe it wasn't a mistake, and that she gave you the wrong number on purpose, but that's obviously not what happened. Anyway, I thought you sounded adorable, so I went to the mall to check you out, and I saw you at the food court across from Victoria's Secret where I knocked over a bra display because I was so nervous, and then I changed my mind about being there because I thought it made me seem like a lunatic stalker, so I went to get coffee, and the next thing I knew, you told me I had a bra stuck to my pants."

I'm out of breath. He is silent. I hope he hasn't hung up.

"We didn't meet by fate that day, Hayden. But once we did meet, I thought you were awesome, and I felt this instant chemistry between us despite the fact that I didn't want a boyfriend. I mean, I *really* liked you. I still do—a lot—and I hope you believe that, and I hope you forgive me for all of this because I only did what I thought I needed to do at the time, even though it was wrong. I know that now, and I'm so sorry."

"This is…I don't understand."

"I know. It's awful. But there's so much more to this than it seems." I take a deep breath and let it out slowly. "I thought you were one of Liv's friends calling me because she wanted me to meet somebody new and so I could go to the dance and make Josh think I've moved on. But when I saw that it wasn't her tricking me and you were a real guy waiting for a real girl, I decided to leave the mall. When we met at Starbucks though, that was real. Once we spoke, I thought, 'I want to get to know him' so I bought a new phone so you could call and text me and not recognize the number."

"You went and bought a new phone?" I can tell he's shocked by all of this. I know I should stop talking, but it's like a faucet's been turned on and my words are water spewing everywhere. Making a giant puddled mess.

"I did. And I knew it was a bad idea, but I wanted to talk to you. And then you texted April. What was I supposed to do?"

"How about not answer it?"

"I know that now. But remember how badly Josh hurt me. And I still wasn't completely sure Liv didn't put you up to this. So I answered."

"Pretending to be her."

I sigh. "I never wanted to lie to you, Hayden."

"But you did."

I deserve that. I don't dispute it. "But then you asked her out. At least, I thought you did. I know now that you were asking for Mark. But then I saw you with her at the mall. I wanted to tell you, I swear I did, because I like you so much, in fact, I think I love you, as crazy as that sounds, but I choked. I was so afraid you'd never want to speak to me again. I can't even blame you if you feel that way now. I messed up. I suck."

There's a gigantic pause. It's like our words dangle between us. It's excruciating.

"Please, say something," I utter.

"I have to go. Bye, Claire." He hangs up.

I'm left with the phone in my hand and tears streaming down my face.

I've ruined the best thing that's ever happened to me before it had a chance to begin.

CHAPTER TWENTY-SIX

I ONLY HAVE a few minutes to cry before Liv texts me that she's here. It's time to go to Mom's salon and get ready for the dance. The dance I don't even want to go to.

But I can't back out now and have Liv mad at me, so I'll go for her, despite that my eyes are a puffy mess and my skin's red and blotchy.

When she comes upstairs to pick me up, I'm still splashing cold water on my face to help lessen the swelling.

It's not working.

After a few minutes, Liv knocks on the bathroom door and speaks through the wood. "Claire, are you all right?"

I open the door, and I can tell by her face that she knows something bad happened. She doesn't say a word, just leans in to hug me. After a few minutes, she lets me go.

"You spoke to Hayden?"

I nod my head and squeeze my eyes shut, but that doesn't prevent two tears leaking from each eye.

Liv hugs me again and rubs my back. I'm full-on crying into her shoulder. I can't help it. My shoulders rise and fall. I gasp for a breath, and all the while, Liv comforts me.

"What did I do?" I say into her shoulder. "I messed everything up. He never wants to see me again."

She lets me cry some more, then she pulls back and hands me a tissue from the dispenser on the bathroom counter. "Did he say that?"

"Not exactly." I blow my nose and toss the balled-up tissue into the trash. "But he was so mad, Liv. You should've heard him. He sounded so disappointed in me and so hurt." That part makes me cry all over again, so Liv hands me another tissue.

"It's going to be all right," she says, but I can tell she might not believe that herself. "Give him time to digest everything. I'm sure he'll call you in a couple of days."

"No, you don't understand." I reach for the hand towel. Tissues aren't going to cut it for me. "It's over," I say, covering my face with the fabric. "I messed this up so bad."

Just when I think there aren't any more tears to shed, more come. I'm a complete, slobbery wet mess. When I finally look back up at her, I see that Liv's eyes are glassy, too.

"He was so mad," I say as I dab my face with the towel and look into the mirror. My face is so swollen from crying that I hardly recognize myself.

"Don't be upset at what I'm about to say." Liv's tone is cautious.

I look at her and wait. I know I was wrong, so I'm going to take my punishment, even if it means my best friend telling me how wrong I was or how much of a fool I still am. Either way, I'm ready.

"He has a right to be mad, and if he is, I don't blame him, so you shouldn't either. He probably feels betrayed."

She's right. I can't even argue.

"*But*," she adds. "He also knows how awesome, caring, sweet, and genuine you are."

"Genuine? I lied to him, Liv. I impersonated someone. That's not genuine, that's deceitful."

"But you meant well, and you said you're sorry. What more can you do?"

I think about that. "There has to be something else I can do."

"Well, I've known you forever and I know for a fact that you'd never do anything to hurt anyone on purpose. If he really likes you, he'll come to realize that, too."

I hope she's right. In my gut, I feel like she's not. I messed up badly. It was the same thing with Josh. I had something good, well, maybe not perfect, but I messed that up with my insecurities and jealousy. Actually, it wasn't exactly the same with Josh. I cared about him, and I thought I loved him. I loved being with him most of the time, and I loved the thought of us being together, and he was cute. But it's different with Hayden. With him, things feel so much more real than they ever did with Josh.

"I told him I loved him. After I confessed everything."

Liv stares. "You did? What did he say?"

"He didn't say anything."

Her expression changes to something like sympathy. It's all I can do not to bolt out of the bathroom sobbing. I swallow another lump in my throat and wait for her reply.

She straightens up suddenly. "Well, it's his loss then. Come on," she says, taking out her phone. "I'm texting Mom that it's going to be a few more minutes."

"Oh my gosh, she's waiting outside?"

"Yeah," she says. "She won't be mad, but we're going to be late for *your* mom at the salon."

"Ugh, do I still have to go to the dance?"

"I think you should. And I'm not just saying that because I want you to, which I do. But wouldn't you rather go and have fun with me rather than sit here crying all day?"

"Now that you put it that way."

"It'll be good for you to get out and forget about stuff for a few hours. Besides, you look too cute in your dress not to go."

I wash my face, and Liv helps get my dress and shoes and make-up together. In a few minutes, we head out for makeovers.

Too bad I can't make over my day.

AT THE SALON, our nails are done first; Liv opts for a French manicure, while I stick with a creamy salmon color. As I wait for mine to dry, I realize I feel a little better since talking to Liv. She's such a great best friend.

Mom does my hair first, cascading curls partly pinned up on the sides and flowing in the back, and then puts Liv's up into a twisted messy side bun with a pretty rhinestone clip secured on top of the bun.

While we're primping, Andy texts me: **Is everything okay with u and Liv now?**

Yes

:) Here too. Thanks for making things right. See u at the dance.

At least I've done one thing right. Maybe two if you count Evan and Leah. If anyone deserves to be happy, it's Liv.

She comes up to me now and, with her phone, snaps a picture of me standing near the shampoo sinks. "You look amazing," she says.

"You do too," I say and take a few shots of her with her phone and then with mine. Every now and then, I start to feel happy, but then my thoughts go back to Hayden and how much I messed up, and my eyes fill up again.

"Stop or your mascara will run," she whispers to me when we're up front, waiting for Dad to pick us up and take us to the school. Mom's so busy with her clients that she hardly notices how upset I really am. Usually, she's on to me. If she's noticed anything today, she probably thinks I'm nervous.

When Dad arrives, he whistles. "Looking good, ladies!"

"Ew, Dad, don't," I say, and he and Liv laugh.

Mom leaves her client to hug us both goodbye, and her coworkers follow. Everyone's oohing and aahing. It makes us laugh, feeling like celebrities.

"Have a great time, beautiful girls," Mom says. "I'll be there by eleven to pick you up."

We slip into Dad's car. I let Liv sit up front. For the entire ride, I'm grateful that they're talking about the latest episode of *Zombified* because I'm in my own head. I stare out the window and think about how I'll never see Hayden again, and there's a pain in my chest way stronger than the one I felt even on that late December night. Right now, I just want to go to bed and stay there for a week—maybe a month.

When we arrive at the school, there's a sea of dressed-up people piling out of cars and into the building. We step onto the curb, and once Dad pulls away, Liv grabs my hand.

"I'm totally here for you," she says. I know she means it. "It'll be okay."

Still, I'm so glad when Andy shows up to take the attention off of me because my eyes are blurred up again and I have to blink a hundred times to keep the tears in.

"Hey, Claire," Andy says, and then he turns to Liv. "You look beautiful."

"Thank you," she says, blushing. He turns to me. "So do you."

I thank him and feel my cheeks warm up, too.

"We have a decoration emergency," he tells Liv and grins. "A display fell over and Madison is freaking out. I tried to help, but she wants you. She said you know exactly how it's supposed to be."

"Go," I say to her. "I'll find you later."

She and Andy take off to fix the problem. I shuffle inside, blending with the crowd and walk toward the gym, which, despite all the Cupids mocking me, looks spectacular. Savory and sweet smells tickle my nose when I enter and a heavy-based 80s club song is playing. Colored lights, mostly red, dance on the walls and ceiling, reflecting off the disco balls in the center and on the hundreds of dangling hearts we slaved over. There are red and white balloons tied with strings of the same colors floating over the tables. A few balloons are loose on the floor, being kicked around by some people, and there is a red and white balloon-arch over the DJ stand. On the back wall, opposite the entry doors, is a huge banner that says 'Welcome to The Cupid Connection Winter Dance!' All over the other three walls are shiny red cut outs of Cupid arching his bow, as well as one hanging off each basketball hoop. Platters of cookies and cakes form tempting rows on the food tables.

The room is filling up already and the DJ changes the song to a grungy 90s song I don't know the name of, but it's one that I like. I wonder if Hayden likes it, too.

Now I'll never know.

I look around and spot Liv and Andy helping Madison with the display she apparently freaked out about. It doesn't look like much—it's a display of props outside a photo booth they rented with the funds they raised. I have to say I'm impressed at how everything looks. If it weren't for the basketball hoops and the shiny wood floor beneath my shoes, I'd never know it was our gym.

A few friends from algebra notice me and call me over, so I go. We say hey and exchange normal school-dance-whatever small talk, but I can't concentrate. As hard as I'm trying not to think about him, Hayden keeps slipping back into my thoughts. Every time he does, my stomach twists and I feel that pain in my chest again as I recall all the stupid things I've done and how hurt he sounded on the phone.

I thought I knew what a broken heart felt like after Josh, but this is worse.

The small crowd breaks up, so I slip away. At one of the snack tables, I pour myself a diet soda, just to have something to hold in my hand, and I'm about to go over to Liv and Andy who have just finished re-propping the prop display when I spot Josh and Briana.

They seem to be having an argument. Josh is gesturing with his hands, his eyebrows creased. Briana gestures back, seeming pissed, too, although she looks gorgeous. She's wearing a red dress that has one long sleeve and leaves the other shoulder bare. Her long black hair cascades in curls down her bare shoulder, and she's wearing black open-toed shoes.

She must have noticed me, because she points in my general direction. I quickly look down at my drink, swirling the ice cubes around in the cup. After a moment, I look back up, planning to seem casual, but it's too late—she's headed toward me.

"Hey, Claire," she says over the music.

"Hi. You okay?" I can't help asking the question, though I'm not sure I want to know the answer.

"Not really. I need to talk to you."

"Okay."

"Can we go somewhere quiet?"

I hope I'm not being set up. The old Briana wouldn't do that. But then again, I never thought she'd steal my boyfriend either.

We walk out of the gym and into the hall near the main entrance. There's a bench off to the side, and she steers us over there. She sits. I remain standing.

"I've wanted to talk to you ever since the other day when you came over to Josh and me."

Somehow, I feel embarrassed. Like maybe I shouldn't have done that. Is she mad? Is she going to tell me off?

"I've been thinking about what you said to me," she says. "I want to tell you how sorry I am. I was wrong. No matter how unhappy you and Josh seemed, I had no right to date him. Even if you had broken up first, it'd be wrong. I was in the moment, and I took the opportunity. I didn't think of your feelings, and I should have. It's just…I always liked him. Don't you remember?"

She's looking at me, and I can tell she's sincere. I think back and things come up in my brain that never, ever clicked before. She *did* tell me and Liv that she liked him. It was back at the beginning of ninth grade. We were at her house for a sleepover.

As if knowing exactly what I'm thinking, she says, "We were in my room. I didn't talk about it much, and one of us changed the subject. I mentioned it a few times after that, but we never really got into it about him. The next thing I knew, that winter, you told me and Liv that you were seeing him. I was devastated."

"So I was the other girl," I say, realizing what had happened.

"Sort of."

How could I have been so wrapped up in myself that I didn't even know I stole the guy she liked right from under her nose? What kind of a friend was I?

Briana looks down at her hands. I sit down beside her. "Bri," I say gently. She looks up; her eyes are glassy but she's keeping her composure. "I'm so sorry. I swear, I didn't remember that until just now. I wish you would have told me when I mentioned I liked him. Or even if you told Liv."

"I tried. But you and Liv always had a way of, I don't know, making me feel like what I said didn't matter as much as what you two talked about."

I feel like I've just been slapped across my face. Is this how I treated her? As if she didn't matter as much as Liv did?

"I am so sorry," I say. My lip quivers as I try not to cry.

Briana bites her bottom lip. Then she hugs me. "I forgive you," she says. "I hope you can forgive me, too."

I hug her back. "None of this would have happened if I'd listened to you. If I'd paid attention. I don't know what else to say."

She releases me.

"Briana, there's something you should know." It takes me a minute to figure out how to say it, the right words to use. I gather my courage. For once, I just spit out the truth. "I'm not sure if Josh is being faithful to you."

Her eyes grow big, but she's speechless.

"He approached me the other day, wanting to talk. I think he wanted more than that. He told me he misses me."

Her eyes dart to the side, and I can tell her mind is going a mile a minute. "I knew it."

"I'm sorry. I just thought you needed to know."

Finally, she looks at me. "You're not glad? This is, like, the best karma ever."

I shake my head. Maybe a week ago I would've been, but not now.

"Thanks for telling me, Claire. I hope we can be friends again. I miss you."

I bite my bottom lip. After a moment, I say, "I miss you, too, and sure, we can be friends again."

I know it won't be like old times. And I know I'll have to convince Liv that this is okay, that Briana's not going to ambush me once she gains my trust back. This whole mess was because of me. I totally see that now. And I see that I really miss my old friend. I can move past it and start over.

And I will. We all will.

CHAPTER TWENTY-SEVEN

I FIND Liv and Andy talking by the punch bowl. Her smile is two miles wide, I swear. I have to scream-whisper in her ear for her to hear me because the music's so loud it's thumping in my chest.

"I had a long talk with Briana!"

"You WHAT? What happened?" she shouts back. Before I can speak, she grabs my wrist and drags me out of the gym. When we get into the hallway, the sudden quiet is deafening. We sneak past the hallway monitors and slip into a classroom where I fill her in on everything that's just happened. At first, she's pissed and untrusting. But then, she recalls times when Briana did seem flustered around Josh.

"It must be true then," she says. "She really told us that she liked him?"

"She did. And we blew her off. We apparently did that to her a lot."

"We never used to take her seriously." I can tell by her frown that Liv feels bad.

"That's because she was always acting silly, like always joking around."

I wonder how hard it must've been for Briana to talk to her

two best friends when they blew off almost every thought she had or comment she made.

"Wow. I guess I should talk to her, too," Liv says.

We slip back into the party. While she goes off to find Briana, I hang out by myself. What a day. I'm physically and emotionally drained. So much so that I think I'm going to call Mom to come and get me early. I'm sure Liv will be okay with that. She and Andy will have a great time, and that's all I really care about now—that, and I think I need a dose of Mooks and my big fluffy comforter. Maybe even another episode of *Zombified*.

I text Mom. She tells me she'll be a little bit because she was in the middle of cooking dinner, and I tell her that's fine, I'll wait. I go to the coat-check to get my coat, and while I'm waiting for it, I text Liv and tell that I'm going home because I'm really tired.

The guy hands me my coat, and I slip it over my shoulders. Then I head toward the main entrance to wait for Mom. It's then that I hear my name. It's Josh again.

I hold up my palm. "Not tonight, Josh."

"I just want to talk for a minute."

"Not again."

"Please. Briana broke up with me. No thanks to you."

"Me?" What nerve he has! "You showed interest in me again, while you're with her, I might add, whom you're with because *you cheated when you were with me*!" I take a deep breath and try to calm myself. "I'm not going over this with you again, Josh. It's over. Have a nice life. Good bye."

I turn away. He grabs my shoulders and turns me to face him.

I try to pull away. "Hey! What are you—?"

"Claire, I still love you. I meant what I said the other day. I know we had our problems, but we have more good memories than bad ones. Don't you ever think about those times? All the good times we had?"

"You can't have a relationship based on memories, Josh. I tried to tell you that the other day. It's not how love works. And you need trust. Now let me go."

"I can make it up to you. I promise you won't regret giving me another chance."

These words should have made me the happiest girl alive. But not now. Now I see that he doesn't know what he wants and that maybe he never did.

I know what I want though.

Just then, he leans in and kisses me. I am immediately brought back to last summer, when things were sweet and good and right. For a split second, I'm fully there, fully immersed in it. Hayden hates me, I tell myself, so it's okay for a second.

But the thing is, it's not okay.

I see Hayden's face in my mind. I love him. I love Hayden, not Josh.

I push Josh away.

Just then, I hear one of the doors open. "Claire?" It's Hayden. He's standing behind me.

The expression on his face says more than any words ever could. I know what this must've looked like. Like I was kissing Josh. Because I was.

I can't deny it. I can't say anything to make it better, but I try anyway. "Hayden, I—"

He turns and leaves, pushing the door with such force it hits the outer wall and then slams closed.

"Hayden! Wait!"

"Forget him, Claire!" Josh says as he tries to stop me.

I pull my arm from Josh's grip and rush out of the double doors, though the parking lot, toward Hayden's jeep. Hayden's striding angrily toward it, his fists clenched. "Hayden!"

He stops mid-step, not turning around, but then continues opening the door and getting into the vehicle.

I take off my heels, toss them aside, and race through the lot, ignoring the sharp pebbles stabbing the bottoms of my feet. If it means keeping Hayden, I'd step on hot coals to reach him right now.

I'm out of breath when I get to the car. He's looking straight ahead, both hands gripping the steering wheel. I stand on my toes and tap the window with the palm of my hand. "Don't go. Please!"

He starts the engine.

"Hayden, please," I say through the closed passenger window. "Josh kissed *me*! I didn't know he was going to do that! You have to believe me!"

He turns to me. Through the window, and even though it's dark out, I see the hurt in his eyes. "Should I believe you, Claire?" he says through the window. "Or is your name April?"

For the second time tonight, I feel like words have slapped me in the face. I can almost feel the handprint.

His face is sad, but his voice is angry. "I saw you kiss him! I know you wanted to take things slow, but you could have been honest with me. You could have told me you were getting back together with your ex. You should have told me the day I picked you up and you were talking to him."

"I was telling him *no* that day. He said he missed me. Before I met you, those words would have meant something. But now... now all I want is to be with you. You have to believe me."

Hayden shakes his head, staring at the steering wheel. "I can't be with someone I don't trust. I know what I saw." He shifts the car in drive.

"Please don't go, not like this."

"Goodbye, Claire." His voice cracks. He raises the window and drives away, leaving me standing in the cold and dark parking lot.

CHAPTER TWENTY-EIGHT

MOM PICKS ME UP, and right away, I know that she knows something's up because she asks me over a hundred times what's wrong. "I can't talk about it right now," I say, and she finally drops the subject. "You let me know when you want to talk," she tells me, which makes me tear up again.

"I will. Thanks, Mom."

Over and over in my mind, the miserable thoughts play. *Why did Hayden show up at the dance? Why couldn't I see this coming? Why couldn't the so-called "real" Cupid drop me a hint? And if Cupid makes all the love connections, why did he make Josh kiss me? Instead of The Cupid Connection, this dance should have been called The Cupid Crisis! Because he doesn't know what he's doing! But maybe it's not Cupid's fault at all. It's mine—based on all my dumb decisions. And I don't deserve Hayden's forgiveness, but I want it so badly.*

When we get home, I text Liv. I fill her in on what has happened, and then I undress and crawl into bed, hugging Mooks.

A few minutes later, Liv calls. Even though I'm too wiped out to talk, I answer.

"You're having the worst week ever," she says.

"I am."

"You all right?"

"No." I fill her in on the details I left out in my text.

"He kissed you? What a dirt bag! And what bad timing for Hayden to show up!"

"I didn't even know he was coming. He was probably going to talk to me. To forgive me. And I blew it again."

"No. That time, it wasn't your fault. Not at all."

I really don't want to talk about it anymore. I have a throbbing headache. "What happened with Briana?" I ask changing the subject. "Did you talk?"

"Yeah. We talked it all out."

"We didn't always listen to her," I say, feeling awful all over again.

"I felt bad about that, too. I never realized how I made her feel."

"Same here."

"But at least Josh helped us to become friends again. That's one thing he's done right."

We laugh at that, but in a small way, I feel bad for him, too. Even though he goes about things the wrong way, he's got feelings, even though they seem to be really mixed up. He just needs to grow up a little, too. Maybe one day he'll be a decent guy and we can be friends. Until then, I'm steering clear of him.

"How was the dance?" I ask. Liv tells me how she and Andy danced during slow songs and how he kissed her in the middle of the dance floor in front of everyone. Hearing her excitement over him makes me happy. And it's good not to be thinking about my troubles for a while.

We talk on the phone until it's half-past midnight and we're both yawning every ten seconds. "I'll see you tomorrow?" Liv says sleepily.

"Okay, tomorrow." My words feel as heavy as my eyelids.

As I drift off to sleep, I realize that even though the day began terribly, and then it got even worse, at least it ended on a positive note.

Maybe things are looking up. I can only hope so.

I MAKE it through the next few days with the help of Liv, Mom, Dad, and even Evan trying to cheer me up, once I was able to tell them what happened without crying.

By Tuesday, I feel a bit better, though not much. The take-home test for English Lit helps keep my mind busy, but I can't concentrate very well because every few minutes, I'm still checking my phone to see if, by some miracle, Hayden called or texted. I'll never know how I managed to finish the test, but eventually I do.

I walk through the halls at school in the haze of a self-pity-party. It's a cycle of sadness followed by self-cheering and posi-tive affirmations, followed again by despair. I need a distraction.

My essay helps as I try to figure out what Shakespeare was thinking when he wrote *A Midsummer Night's Dream*. So many characters! So much deception! So much confusion and drama! It's also funny to me, especially the part where Bottom gets a donkey head and Titania falls for him. Plus, Robin Goodfellow, a.k.a. Puck, puts spells on the wrong people after the cameo appearance of Cupid, who put the love potion in the flower to begin with.

And then there's poor Helena.

At first, when I thought about her, she made me sad. She was so insecure. Then I got mad and wanted to shake her. Like, *stop it, woman! Put on your big girl pants and move on!* And then I felt sorry over how pathetic it got, with both men liking her and her thinking they were mocking her. Really, it was the magic. They didn't really like her, either of them. I still think it's sad how she didn't think more highly of herself. If I were to meet her today as a real person, I'd help her develop some self-confidence.

I finished my essay over the weekend, adding the ending:

Lord Tennyson said that it's better to have loved and lost than to never have loved at all. I'm not sure Shakespeare would have said the same thing, because Shakespeare himself said that love is blind. He also said that the course of true love never did run smooth. This seems truer to me. Love almost always ends in heartache. So why would it be best to have loved and then lost? So it could hurt doubly? Maybe he should have said that we're all better off never loving anyone. I mean, why would anyone want to be in love and endure that kind of torture? Or maybe Tennyson had never been in love and Shakespeare had. That had to be it. Maybe Tennyson tried to find love, but it never came to him; it was always an arm's length away. Or maybe he tried once. Maybe he poured his heart out the way Helena did with Demetrius, but maybe he had his heart broken in return. Maybe he made a mistake and tried to apologize for the things he'd done, but it didn't matter. Because the truth is, once you make a mistake, it's over. People don't always forgive. They leave. Some cheat. Love isn't worth it.

So in conclusion, if I had one thing to say to Helena, it'd be RUN. Run far away and live alone. Get some cats. Or gerbils. Or whatever. It doesn't matter because you'll probably end up hurt and alone anyway. And to Demetrius, I'd say, "You're a fool. You didn't even know what you had and you let it flit away like a wayward butterfly."

ON WEDNESDAY, I put Mooks in my closet. I can't get rid of him. But I can't look at him either. I throw the new phone into the recycling bin. It's time to move on. Hayden isn't going to call. I turn my old cell off and stick it in my side-table drawer because I have to train myself to stop looking at it every ten seconds. Still, the knowledge that Hayden isn't returning my texts sits like a sad lump in my gut.

It's late when Evan knocks on my bedroom door and peeks in. "Claire?"

"What." I'm lying on my bed, staring at the ceiling, having an imaginary talk with Helena, who's telling me to snap out of it. Yeah, I know, I'm going crazy.

Evan comes in and stands over me, frowning. He puts his hands on his hips. "Snap out of it," he says.

"*That* was weird," I say. Of course, he has no idea what I mean, and I'm too tired to explain it.

"I mean it, Claire. Get up and do something."

"Why?" I lift my head in order to see the time on my alarm clock. "It's almost 11:00. What do you want me to do?"

"I don't mean right now." Evan sighs and folds his arms across his chest. There's a definite look of concern on his face. "I know you're sad about Hayden, but you're not really getting over it, and it reminds me of when you and Josh broke up."

Aw, he cares.

"You helped me with Leah, so I want to help you. So I've been thinking. I might know what you have to do to get him to forgive you."

"And what's that?"

"You have to go big. It has to *matter*." He points at me, leaning closer. "If you want to get him back, you have to do something big—step out of your comfort zone in a huge way. You have to show him you care."

"Evan, I've done all I could do. I texted, called, and ran across the parking lot in my bare feet. Nothing I said or did mattered. So thanks for trying to help me, but this one's hopeless. It's over."

Evan shakes his head. "If I didn't take your advice, I wouldn't be with Leah."

"And if you didn't take my advice, she wouldn't have broken up with you."

"True. But you helped me fix it. You knew what to do. You always know what to do. Even if it takes two attempts, or three. *Or more.* If you love him, you have no choice."

"Well, I don't have the answers this time, so..."

"You know that's a lie."

"Lying's what I do best, apparently."

"You're being stubborn."

"You sound like Mom."

"No, I sound like *you*. One time, you told me that actions speak louder than words. I don't remember why you said it, but I always remember it because it was true then and it's true now. And, by the way, running in bare feet counts as going big, but that's not big enough. Just saying."

I stare at him.

"Anyway, you know I'm right. Just think about it." Evan turns and leaves, and I spend the next hour thinking about what he just said, basically because I can't think of anything else, no matter how hard I try.

Surprising even to myself, thinking about Evan's words actually gives me an idea. One that might work.

I slip under my blanket and turn on my side. I'm almost asleep when a thought occurs to me, making me giggle. *Evan's pretty smart—for an Internet meme.*

CHAPTER TWENTY-NINE

IT'S DO *or die* time. It's Friday, and even though my plan isn't perfect, I spent all day yesterday figuring out the details, mapping it out. I discovered there's an event tonight at the mall, and I'm determined to go through with trying to win Hayden back. To do whatever it takes. To go big. He's working tonight so it's now or never.

By eighth period English class I'm antsy to get things going and rethinking all the details of my plan when Ms. Levine hands back our now-graded essays. I glance down at mine. I got an A- with a note in red ink in the top corner: *Great job. See me after class.*

I wonder what she wants to talk to me about.

"You wanted to see me?" I ask once everyone's left. Ms. Levine's back is to me; she's wiping off the smart board.

She turns around. "Yes, Claire. I wanted to tell you that I loved your take on *A Midsummer Night's Dream.* I especially loved your perspective on Helena. Good job."

"Thanks."

"I also wanted to make sure you're okay. Are you?"

"Oh, yeah." My cheeks burn. "I guess I kind of had personal experiences to draw from. I hope it wasn't too much."

"Well, it was a bit too informal, but it was fine. *This time*." Ms. Levine smiles. "At least your experiences served you well in English class. Good writing. Now go, before you miss your bus."

I thank her again and head out. An A-minus! Awesome.

On the bus, I think more about the last-minute details of my plan. "Go big," Evan had said. And he was right. So that's what I'm about to do. It may not work, but if Shakespeare could turn people into donkeys for the purpose of love, I can purchase a few props for mine.

So when I get home, I gather all my saved up birthday/Christmas money, eighty-two dollars to be exact, and stash it in my purse. I reach for my jacket, and before I leave, I find Evan in the kitchen where he's dunking Oreos into a tall glass of milk.

"I'm taking the bus to the mall," I tell him. "But first I'm going to Wal-Mart. I have to pick up a couple of things there."

Evan looks up from his bowl. Milk drips from his chin. He chews, swallows, and then says, "Going big?"

"Yeah. I just hope it's big enough." I pause and look at my little brother. "Oh and thanks."

"No prob." More chewing, slurping.

"You're gross."

Evan shows me a mouthful.

"Ew. Tell Mom I'll be home after dinner sometime and not to worry."

"'K. Good luck," he mumbles.

"I've heard *that* before."

I TAKE the bus to Wal-Mart. I've got about fifteen minutes to buy what I need and get back outside in order to make the next bus to the mall. I rush to the toy section. I go up and down every aisle until I find what I need: a giant monkey and a bullhorn. I pay for them and then rush back out into the cold to wait for the bus.

I need two seats once I get on, and thankfully there are two together. I ignore the stares from fellow passengers and pray that my plan works. According to the time on my phone, Hayden should already be at work. I hope he hasn't called in sick.

I chose today to set my plan into action once I read in yesterday's newspaper that there was going to be a small senior citizen fashion show right outside one of the big department stores, which is right next to The Photo Shoot. I took it as a sign and figured it would be my last-ditch effort to get Hayden to hear me out and realize how sorry I am. The article said that some of the photographers from his job will be there, taking photos. I just hope he's one of them.

My hands are clammy and my throat is dry as I carry my props, struggling to balance it all. The monkey is practically as big as me. Between it in one arm and my purse hanging off the other arm, that's also carrying the bullhorn, I can hardly see in front of me, which makes me even more nervous. I can't back out now though. Do or die. And as much as I wanted to call Liv and bring her with me for support, I knew I had to do this alone. Plus, doing it alone would hopefully make more of an impact, since Hayden knows how much I fear speaking in public.

There are more stares from passersby, and the mall is busier now than usual. I reach the stage. Behind it, I see dolled-up senior women wearing shimmery jewelry and sequined gowns.

"Wow, honey, that monkey's bigger than you," one woman says. "Do you need a hand?"

"Oh, thanks," I say, peering at her from behind it. "I'm okay." Right then, I get another idea. At first, I was going to stand outside of The Photo Shoot and speak to Hayden from there. But now I think I'll try something even better, *bigger*. "But, uh, do you think you could help me with something else?" I ask.

"Sure, what's that?"

I whisper in her ear and give her the short version of what I've come to do, and then I tell her my new idea. When I'm done, she smiles at me, her rosy cheeks turning rosier. "Oh! Young love! It's so magical!"

"So you'll help me?"

"Well, it's a mighty tall order, but it's for a good cause." She leans closer to me and whispers. "I'll see what I can do. Wait over there, honey." She winks and points to the side of The Photo Shoot entryway, where I told her Hayden works.

I stand on the side of the stage and wait for her cue. Music begins a few minutes later, and a crowd is seated in the folding chairs, clapping and waiting for the show to begin. There are a few photographers snapping pictures already, but none of them is Hayden. I look over and spot him in The Photo Shoot, speaking to someone. I hope he doesn't see me. Not yet.

On the stage, a man in a tuxedo steps up to the mic and taps it, getting everyone's attention. The applause quiets, and with the new silence, my heart is in my throat. I know the time for me to act is fast approaching.

"Welcome to the tenth annual Senior Fashion Frenzy!" he says, and applause erupts again. My stomach twists and turns. I swallow hard. I might pass out right here.

"We've got a great night planned for you with the latest fashion from designer Katie Bee, straight from her boutique on Ninth Avenue." More applause, some whooping. "Let's give a big hand for, oh…what's this?"

The kind woman I spoke to is up on stage, whispering in his ear.

The MC clears his throat and loosens his tie. "It seems there's a glitch we need to work out backstage. Please give us a moment." There is murmuring in the audience as he steps off the stage. The kind woman winks and nods toward the mic. It's my cue.

I swallow a larger lump in my throat and take the monkey and bullhorn with me. I climb up the steps, onto the stage. I stand in front of all these people. My legs shake. My insides quiver. I might even throw up.

The audience, the newspaper people, and the photographers have gone silent and seem confused as to what's caused the show to stall. I stand at the mic, clear my throat, and stare at the sea of confused faces before me. My entire body stiffens. I can't find my words, and my mouth is dry, but I can't back down now. *Do or die, Claire. Go big.*

I tap the mic. The feedback squeals loudly, and I step back a little. I don't need the bullhorn but I hold it in my right hand anyway. I balance the monkey on my left hip.

"This is—" I say into the mic, but it's still too loud and screeches with more feedback. Some people cover their ears. I step back and try again. "This is for Hayden," I say without the shrilling sound. "Hayden at The Photo Shoot."

I point, sort of, with the horn in my hand. Though confused, everyone looks in the direction of the store. Someone must have gone to get him, because he appears at the entryway a moment later. One of his coworkers points at me and Hayden's expression changes from confused to recognition. We lock eyes.

Now or never.

I lean toward the mic again and clear my throat. "This is for you, Hayden," my voice booms. I hear the massive pounding of my heartbeat in my ears and a few people hushing others as I force the words to come out despite the paralysis threatening to steal my voice and send me running offstage.

"I made a mistake," I say, my voice shaking. "More than one, actually. But I'm standing here to tell you how sorry I am." *Focus on him,* I tell myself as my whole body shivers. *Don't focus on the crowd and all those eyes looking at you. You can do this. Do it for him.*

Hayden stares back at me. For some reason, this is making me more nervous. Behind me, I hear shuffling. I have to move quickly.

"I don't know if you'll ever forgive me for everything I've

done, but I hope you'll understand that I'm truly sorry," I say.

There's more commotion backstage, and I hear a woman's voice talking over a man's. I'm guessing it's the MC and the woman who gave me this chance. I hope she doesn't get kicked out of the show. I glance over my left shoulder and see two security guards coming up the steps toward me.

Now or never!

I speak fast. "The times I spent with you were the best I've ever known. You made me feel special. Most of all, you showed me that it's okay to love someone again and to trust again. I'm sorry I betrayed *your* trust. I never meant to hurt you, Hayden. So today, right now, I am here to tell you I'm truly sorry and I hope you can forgive me. Please, forgive me." I lift the monkey higher. "And what better way is there to show someone you love them? With a giant monkey, of course."

The crowd cheers and claps. The guards approach me and grab my arms. I hope Hayden realizes how hard this was for me. But there's no way of knowing what his reaction is to what I'd just done because when I search for his face again, I can't find it.

Once again, Hayden is gone.

Defeated, I drop the bullhorn and monkey right on the stage. The next thing I know, the guards escort me by my elbows down the steps. I don't fight them. As we pass the kind woman, she frowns and mouths, "I'm sorry."

Behind me, the MC apologizes to the crowd for my rude interruption, but they boo him. One person, a man, yells, "Let her go!" and then another, a woman, agrees and says, "Forgive and forget, Hayden!"

All around me, photographers are snapping pictures, and I know they're of me being led off the stage and not of the fashion show, which the MC is now desperately trying to begin.

"What did you think you were doing up there?" says the guard who is gripping my left arm.

"Do you know how much trouble you're in, young lady?"

growls the other.

I'm surprised I'm not in handcuffs, but I don't care about the trouble coming to me. I don't think Hayden was moved at all by what I'd done. All I managed was to look like a fool. I'm sure I'll be on the front page of the local paper tomorrow. The headline will probably read: *Senior Fashion Frenzy Marred by Teen Girl's Monkey Business.*

I also don't care that I've left my purse behind. I don't care about anything. I'm told to call my parents to come and get me. I can't get in touch with Mom, so I try Dad. When I reach his office, his secretary tells me he's coming, but he was in an important meeting, so he will try to cut it short. I feel terrible. While I wait, the mall cops interrogate me.

"What was your plan once you got up on the stage?"

"To do what I did—apologize to Hayden."

"Who is Hayden? Was he in on this, too?"

"He's my boyfriend. Well, now he's my ex. And was he in on what?"

"The plan."

"The plan to *apologize to him*? No!"

"No need to be snarky, miss."

"Sorry, but some of these questions are—"

"Did you have something else up your sleeve?"

"I had a bullhorn and a monkey. What else could I have possibly been holding?" I don't say it, but I think these mall cops take their jobs way too seriously.

"Again with the snark. Did you pay for those things? Was that a stolen monkey?"

"Of course I paid for them. Where's my dad?"

Dad arrives almost an hour later, having been caught in traffic. I'm exhausted by their dumb, endless questions. Mostly, I'm angry with myself. I feel like a criminal. But as soon as I look up at Dad's face, which is first angry and then full of sympathy, I get up, hug him, and cry into his jacket.

CHAPTER THIRTY

I WAIT for Dad in the car while he signs papers banning me from the mall for one month, and while he retrieves my purse, bullhorn, and monkey. When he gets to the car, I take my purse but ask if we can find a trash can to throw out the rest. "I don't even want to look at those things."

"If we see one on the way home, I'll stop," Dad says, but we never see one. All the way home, I'm in tears and I can't look at him and I know he must feel badly because he's not even lecturing me about how irresponsible I was, or how I took him away from a big meeting with potential buyers for the Landry estate. His secretary told me that when I was forced to call from the security office.

By the time we get to our street, my face is soaked with tears. Dad pulls over a few houses from ours.

"Why'd you stop?" I ask while wiping my eyes with my sleeves.

Dad turns off the engine. "Claire Bear," he says softly. I feel the tears building back up. "Talk to me. What happened?"

I grab a napkin from the stash he keeps in the glovebox and blow my nose.

He takes my hand in his and rests them on the gear shift. "I'm not *that* mad at you."

I look at him, the napkin still over my nose. "You're not? Not even for flubbing the Landry estate purchase?"

He shakes his head. "It's not flubbed."

I'm relieved. But still sad.

"What you did was wrong, sure. But it was also sweet. And brave."

"You don't think I made a total ass of myself?"

"No. What you did was act on pure feelings. Which isn't always the best way to handle things. But I get it. You should have thought things through a little more, like maybe found a way to do your demonstration without interrupting an event other people had planned. Does that make sense?"

I shrug. "I don't know. But I do know that I made a total fool of myself. I can never show my face there again."

"Well, not for a month, at least."

I playfully tag his arm. "Ha-ha. Very funny."

"I think it was sweet, what you did. Although the people at the fashion show might be peeved. I'd be too if I were running the show."

"You should have seen the MC's face," I say nodding. "Hayden must've been laughing at me. He probably hates me."

"I'm sure he doesn't hate you. You'll see, one day you'll laugh over this."

"I never will."

"Don't be too sure. You know, I did something similar with your mom once. About twenty years ago."

I look over at him, shocked. My parents never fight.

"She broke up with me. She gave me the engagement ring back and everything."

"She broke up after you were engaged?"

"It was a pre-engagement ring, since we were still in high school."

Like the promise ring from Josh.

"But to me," Dad continues, "it meant fully engaged. I loved her with all my heart."

"That's so cheesy, Dad."

"Maybe. But love makes you do dumb things."

"Tell me about it."

He smiles, and I can tell he's reliving the whole story as he tells me the rest. "We broke up over my being jealous of her talking to some kid on the swim team."

That's what I did with Josh. I guess I'm more like Dad than I thought.

"It was dumb, but I was in love with her. I didn't want her talking to any guy. So I forbade her to."

I turn fully in my seat to face him. "You *forbade* her? Dad!"

"I know, I know. She didn't speak to me or take my calls for two weeks. I was devastated. Couldn't eat; couldn't sleep; nothing."

"I know the feeling."

"Stinks, doesn't it?"

"Yeah," I say. "Love stinks."

At that, he belts out a few lines of the song, which makes me laugh.

"So anyway...it was during a football game we had one weekend. I played quarterback. I knew she'd be in the stands with her friends, so I came up with the idea to apologize in front of everyone in order to show her how serious I was. There were hundreds of students in the bleachers. So, right before the game started, I got down on my knee on the grass, held a hand over my heart, and announced to her in front of everyone how sorry I was. I begged for her to forgive me."

I laugh again, picturing him. "Did she?"

"No. She ran off, embarrassed. She's petrified of crowds watching her."

I guess I get that trait from her.

"Boy, did I get it from my coach. I was benched that night for holding up the game. He was so mad. It seemed everyone was mad at me, not to mention how humiliating it was to be made fun of by the rest of the team. Heck, by the entire school. I was known after that, and for a long time, as Sorry-Sam."

"Sorry-*Sam*? That's not even your name!"

"It was after that," he says, laughing.

"Oh my God, Dad, that's hysterical!" It kind of reminds me of Nick Bottom in Shakespeare's play—the guy with the donkey head, the one who looked like a fool.

"Sometimes your mom still calls me that," he says. "When she's mad at me."

"You'll never live this down. You know that, right?"

He sighs dramatically, making his cheeks puff out. Then he says, "Well, I haven't lived it down yet. But my point is it was my true feelings that made her change her mind. The following day, she showed up at my job. She said she needed time to think about what I'd said, and how I'd said it, and how sweet she thought I was to do that in front of so many people. Then she accepted my apology. We've been together ever since."

"Wow, that's awesome, Dad."

"Yeah. So I wanted to tell you that what's meant to be will be."

"I appreciate that," I say. "But I don't think Hayden and I are meant to be. I did a lot to hurt him. To ruin his trust. I blew it."

I grab another napkin as new tears fall down my cheeks.

"I think you may be wrong about that," he says. I look up to see him pointing toward our house. I squint, and through the darkening night, I can see that there's a jeep parked at the curb. It's Hayden. And he's standing in our driveway.

CHAPTER THIRTY-ONE

"Want me to drive away?" Dad asks with a grin, and I know he's kidding. But the way I look right now, I'm not sure Hayden will want to see me.

"Can I fix my face a little first?"

"You look perfect, honey. I'm sure Hayden would agree."

"Thanks, Dad." Despite that, I rummage through my purse for lip gloss, some compact powder and a little blush. A few seconds later, I'm done. My heart is full-on thrashing.

"You ready?"

"Yeah."

Dad turns the car back on and pulls up in the driveway. Hayden has been waiting, leaning on Mom's car this whole time. Was he going to wait all night for me? Dad turns off the engine. I get out of the car, and Hayden says hello to him and then to me.

Dad waves good night and goes inside the house. Once we're alone, Hayden suggests we get into the jeep.

"It's warmer. Maybe we can ride around and talk?"

"Sure." I climb in, my hands shaking so badly that I have to sit on them.

"Cold?" he asks, nodding toward my hands.

"A little."

We don't talk much at first. It's mostly about the heat being too high or too low.

Finally, I blurt, "I'm so sorry about everything."

At the same time, he says, "I'm sorry I didn't give you a chance."

We laugh as we both start and stop at the same time again. Then he holds up one hand and says, "You go first. I'll listen."

"I'm not sure there's much else to say, only that I truly am sorry, Hayden. I meant every word I said before. I got in too deep, and I didn't know how to get out of it. Especially when I realized how much I liked you."

"Understandable."

"Is it?"

"Yeah. I mean, once I thought about it, it all seemed a little funny. I think it'll be one of those stories we'll laugh about years later."

I think of Dad's story. They probably laugh about it all the time, picturing Dad on the field, on his knee, one hand on his heart like some Shakespearean actor in a play.

"I did show up with a bullhorn."

"And a giant monkey." He's snickering now.

"Well, you said there's no better way to show your love than with a giant monkey, didn't you?"

"I sure did. And you spoke in front of that huge crowd." He glances sideways at me. "I'm surprised you didn't pass out."

"I almost did."

"So I guess you really did mean it, then. All those things you said."

"Every single word."

Hayden drives some more, and the only sound in the car is the radio announcer talking about some huge car sale. When we pull up at my house again, we idle in the driveway, the heat full blast.

"So…now what?" I say.

Hayden leans across the gear shift and turns my face toward his. "So now, *this*."

His kiss is slow, deliberate. Every cell in my body awakens. I am warm all over, and it isn't because of the heat blowing in my face. I wrap my free arm around him, my hand resting on his neck, my fingers threading through his hair. He kisses me for a long time. His lips are soft and his touch softer. I'm sorry when he stops.

He rests his forehead on mine. I look into his eyes. "I really am sorry."

"Shh." He places his finger on my lips. "We don't have to talk about it anymore. We'll save it so we can laugh about it, let's say, one year from today. It'll be Saturday, February 20th." He looks at the time display on the dash. "At 10:42 P.M."

"It's a date," I say.

He kisses me again, but all too soon, it's time for me to go inside. "It's late. My mom's blinking the porch light."

Hayden looks up. "Yup, she is."

"So annoying."

"It's all right. We have tomorrow."

"And the day after that?"

"And the day after *that*."

I lean in for one last kiss before I hop out of the jeep.

"Can I ask you something?" he says. "Where's the monkey?"

"In my dad's car. I was about to toss it, but we couldn't find a dumpster. Why?"

"I was hoping you didn't leave it at the mall or get rid of it. Can I keep it?"

"Sure. I'll get it now."

I grab it from Dad's car and set it in Hayden's passenger seat, buckling it into the seatbelt.

Hayden laughs. "He's awesome. And he needs a name."

"Mooks the Second?" I offer.

"I think he needs something more unique to him. To commemorate his purpose on this planet. He sort of brought us together again."

I think for a moment. "What about Cupid?" I say.

"Perfect." Hayden pats Cupid's round belly. "I hope I don't get a ticket for driving a giant monkey around."

"If I didn't get one for interrupting a senior fashion show, you should be fine."

"True," he says. "But you *were* arrested by the mall cops."

"And banned from the mall for a month."

"Hey, look at that," he laughs. "I'm seeing an ex-con!"

"Ha-ha." I lean across Cupid for one last kiss good night before Hayden backs out of the driveway.

I watch the taillights fade down the street. As I take a step toward the front porch, something catches my eye, a flicker of white light. I turn and glance around, but nothing is there.

After a moment, I sigh, thinking of all that has changed for me since December 27th. I feel lucky and grateful that I met Hayden, and I'm glad that I was able to fix what almost cost me that relationship. I giggle now, thinking of the giant monkey tonight at the mall. I'm proud of myself for facing my fears, too.

I picture Cupid again, one last time, sitting on the hood of Dad's car. He's holding a tiny bullhorn in his own chubby hand. But this time, instead of imagining conking him over the head with it, I just laugh and thank him. "Really. Thanks, dude. You were right all along," I say out loud.

Just as I'm about to go inside, I see the tiny flickering light again. It flits like a firefly. *That's weird,* I think to myself. *There are no fireflies in February.* I squint, but in an instant, the light disappears.

I look around my now-dark front yard and shiver. It's too cold to stand here and wonder what that was, so I shrug it off, and slip inside. Then, taking two steps at a time, I race up to my room so I can call Liv.

And maybe Briana.

ACKNOWLEDGMENTS

A huge thank you to Brookie Cowles and the Literary Crush Publishing team for believing in this book and for taking a chance on me. Thank you to Arielle Bailey—editing is your superpower.

I must acknowledge Jennifer Salvato Doktorski for not only being one of my best friends, but for being an amazing critique partner. Your insights and writing ability are second to none.

To my talented critique group, thank you from the bottom, top, and all sides of my heart for supporting me while writing this book. This includes: Renee Doboy, Aliza Schauder, Rajdeep Paulus, Selene Castrovilla, and Jamie Hutter. Thank you for reading ten million versions of this story and for putting up with my tantrums while doing so. To Annette Kaelin, thanks for being so supportive and for reading all those pages on the plane rides!

A special thanks goes to Emily Hawe for introducing me to *A Midsummer Night's Dream* and for all the ideas that followed.

To my loving, supportive, I-can't-ask-for-anyone-better husband, Mike: All I can say is thank you for always having my back. I love you. To the greatest kids on the planet, Steven and Julianna, I love you both more than any words I can write on this page. To my parents, Roseanne and Joe Buscemi, my sister Lori, my brother Joe, my in-laws, friends, and co-workers who have been on this journey with me: You have always believed in me, all these years. That is *everything*.

Last but definitely not least, thank you, God, for guiding me along this path. I'm humbled.

ABOUT THE AUTHOR

As a kid, Lisa Buscemi Reiss disliked reading, but loved stories. It wasn't until sixth grade when she won her elementary school's Creative Writing award that she realized her true love of writing. Now she writes middle grade and teen fiction hoping to inspire future writers and readers. She loves the beach and the sun, and is married to a handsome guy she met when they were teenagers. They now have two amazing, talented, cool kids, a dog, and two cats and live in Long Island, NY. *The Cupid Crisis* is her debut novel.

Learn more about her at: LisaBuscemiReiss.com

MORE BOOKS BY LITERARY CRUSH PUBLISHING

Sleigh Ride: A Seasonal Romance Anthology

Kissing in the Rain: A Seasonal Romance Anthology

April Showers: A Seasonal Romance Anthology

Emmie and the Tudor King (Coming June 2019)

The Engagement Contract (Coming July 2019)

CPSIA information can be obtained
at www.ICGtesting.com
Printed in the USA
BVHW081255110319
542310BV00008B/648/P